ELIJAH'S
Want

SHARK'S EDGE: BOOK EIGHT

VICTORIA BLUE

ELIJAH'S
Want

SHARK'S EDGE: BOOK EIGHT

VICTORIA BLUE

WATERHOUSE PRESS

Dearest David, you are all the things
I could ever Want. I love you. SS

CHAPTER ONE

ELIJAH

An entire month had come and gone since we learned about the Trasks being granted early release by the parole board.

Hannah was inconsolable for a good hour or two of that first day. But then, in true warrior fashion, she plastered on that damn cheer competition smile of hers and started spouting catchphrases about things being tough, so we needed to stay focused and be tough too.

I put a fast end to that bullshit by covering her mouth with mine and devouring every square inch of her perfection. She could act as tough as she wanted, but I felt her body tremble from the top of her honey-blond head to the bottom of her ticklish, sexy toes. She wasn't fooling me.

I was so obsessed with the woman it frightened me. I wanted to spend every single moment of the day with her. Inside her. Learning about her and learning about myself through her eyes. And my hope for her was that she would come to understand that, together, we could take on anything life put in our path. Because I was already pretty damn sure this woman belonged by my side, and we made an incredible team.

To all my musings, I only had one summarizing thought.

Hensley *who*?

Even if nothing permanent developed between Hannah and me, she'd given me that incredible gift. No one before her had accomplished that mission, and I owed her so much gratitude for setting me free from the shackles of that woman's memory.

Daily, I fought the urge to tell her how I felt. I was in love with her. My feelings were not confused or mistaken. I was certain she was the woman I'd be content spending the rest of my life with. But every time the reckless notion to tell her made its way to the forefront of my mind, it got lost in the mix of whatever conversation I was doing my best to pay attention to. The woman jumped from topic to topic like she was playing mental hopscotch on a hot tin roof. In Arizona. On a summertime lunch break.

Much like the one we were having at this very moment.

"Has Sebastian said anything about wanting more children?" Hannah asked out of the blue.

We were sharing takeout Chinese from white cardboard boxes while seated around the living room coffee table.

I chuckled, remembering the conversation my best friends and I had when Bas said he wanted to have another child as soon as possible. I didn't think sharing the spiteful reason why would paint him in a favorable light to Hannah though, so I kept that part to myself when I answered. He dug deep enough holes on his own and didn't need anyone else's help.

"I've heard him say he wants a bunch of kids. I guess he and Abbigail both do," I answered while poking around with my chopsticks, looking for another mushroom in the stir-fry. "Why do you ask?"

"Abbi's been acting a little off this week. But I thought it might be my perception since I've been feeling overly tired and a little anxious myself." She paused for a moment and then added, "But I'm pretty sure I heard her getting sick in the bathroom this morning."

I probably should've concentrated harder on keeping a poker face in place, but by the time I tried to play it off and said something to head Hannah off that thought track, I was already grinning.

"Oh, you know something you're not telling me!" With that comment, she dropped her chopsticks with a little clatter and launched her entire body into me, knocking us both backward until she straddled my lap in the most delicious way.

"Woman," I growled and pushed my growing cock up into her. "Be glad you have on jeans, or I'd be giving you a quick lesson on how babies are made."

"I don't know, Mr. Banks," she said, and circled her pelvis on top of mine. "I've attended your lessons in the past. They're anything but quick."

"Have you made an appointment with your doctor?" Yes, it was a bit of a buzzkill. Not a full mood destroyer, but I was so over suiting up every time I wanted inside this woman's body. "You mentioned you were going to do it last week, but I never heard anything more about it."

"I keep meaning to, but I always have time at the wrong time, you know? Too early in the morning, or when"—Hannah let her head fall back on her shoulders, and a husky moan tore up her throat—"God yes, right there. That's what I need, mmm, so good."

Quickly, I wrapped her hair around my wrist until my fist was full of her blond tresses. I sat up so our torsos were

3

pressed together and held her close by the impromptu leash I just made.

Between kisses and sharp bites down her exposed neck, I asked, "Do you want *me* to call? Or I can have Carmen make the appointment."

"Elijah!"

"What?" Clearly, I was missing something based on the deafening tone she just used.

"Your assistant is not making my gynecology appointment for me." She leaned back, balancing all her weight on my completely stiff shaft and cradling her face in both hands. "Oh my God, I'd be mortified."

My brain short-circuited. Flatlined. Just black-and-white confetti, like the television screen when the cable went out. Every single thought, breath, and heartbeat was focused on that exact place where my dick and her pussy were grinding together through our pants.

"Fuck. Me. Girl. What are you fucking doing to me?" I let go of her hair to grip her hips instead. I didn't want the exquisite torture to stop.

Hannah tilted her chin toward the ceiling and slid both open palms seductively down her throat and across her collarbones. Then, just as she skimmed over her breasts, I issued some directions.

"Stop there."

She had finally figured out that doing what I wanted— what I told her, instructed, commanded, demanded she do— ended so much better than when she defied me. That wasn't to say she didn't still push my patience from time to time. I wouldn't have it any other way, though. I loved her feisty spirit as much as I loved her docile obedience.

Luck was on my side at the moment because, apparently, she was feeling obedient. She also just happened to have on a button-down shirt that I made quick work of unfastening from the bottom toward the top until my large hands met her much smaller ones where she still cupped her tits.

"Let me see, beautiful. Take this off. The bra too."

But when I saw the bra covering her peachy skin, I changed my mind.

"No. Wait. Leave the bra."

Hannah brought her chin level once more and squinted at me. "Make up your mind, chief."

"Watch yourself," I issued, and the brat actually had the courage to roll her eyes. Okay, clearly I'd gone too easy on her.

"Oh, darling. Shouldn't have done that."

"You don't scare me," she taunted.

"We could change that. It wouldn't take much to have you begging for me to stop."

Of course, my cock loved the direction the conversation had turned. It had been a while since I'd gone down any dark alleys. In truth, I wouldn't mind dragging Hannah into the shadows now and then. At the same time, I didn't want to scare her, and I'd done some depraved things in my day that would do exactly that.

Just take baby steps, whispered the devil on my shoulder.

You'll lose the best thing that's ever happened to you, argued the angel perched on the other side.

I used to believe I had a devil on both sides. So many women let me do whatever I wanted to their bodies and came back for more. But when Hannah came into my life, I realized I didn't want all that darkness—at least not all the time. This was the first time I'd even felt like I'd been missing it. My behavior had become more of a habit than a craving. Or at least that was what I had been telling myself. But it seemed like a reasonable explanation.

When Hensley betrayed me, I was so hurt. I wanted to strike out at the entire female population as a whole, and not just the woman who caused my pain. It was easier to tell myself that all women were the same—heartless and vindictive—than to try to sift through the masses and find the potential diamond in the rough.

I had put my time in with her, and what did I have to show for it? A broken heart, an empty bed and bank account, and a constant need to look over my shoulder.

So I vowed to never trust a woman again. Never be duped into believing my one true love was out there searching for me while I was searching for her. Knowing that when we found each other, we would just know. Our two pieces would recognize that we'd found our other half and we'd be together forever. Because, as crazy as it sounded, that was what I believed before she steamrolled over my heart and soul with her malicious, evil, lying, cheating cruelty.

Damn—I gave her everything I had. Including my entire truth.

"Is that right?" Hannah challenged, jutting her chin with more defiance.

"What's gotten into you? All this sass—not like you, beautiful."

I startled a quick yip from her when I pushed her flat beneath me and straddled her lap with my body. I looked down at my pretty captive while her chest worked up and down with every breath she drew in and let out.

"Now, what should we do about this attitude, Ms. Farsey?"

I raked my gaze from her bright-blue eyes down the full length of her body and back again. Growling low in my throat, I said, "Fuck me, this bra is so sexy," and plucked at her tight nipple through the sheer fabric of one of the cups.

Black lace with lavender satin accents made the sweetest temptation of lingerie I might have ever laid eyes on. Of course, the fact that it caressed Hannah's flawless ivory skin might have been the precise detail that made it so special.

"Tell me, baby. Are there matching panties hiding under these jeans?"

While asking the question, I roughly tugged at the button and zipper of her pants. When she shot her hands out to stop my progress, I lifted a brow in warning.

"Pardon me?" I issued.

Hannah stared up at me, not saying a word, but I didn't miss the rough swallow she worked down her throat. At the same time, she maintained the grip she had around my wrist, hampering my movement.

"Are you shy tonight? Do you need something useful to do with your hands right now?" I pointedly looked down at where she was gripping mine.

I couldn't resist the plump invitation of her mouth for another minute. I crowded over her with my body and devoured her lips. Stealing her breath and replacing it with my desire, I stabbed into the recess of her willing mouth with my tongue, tempting and tasting her until we were both breathless.

In the cradle of my large palms, I maneuvered her face to my liking, angling her for the deepest exploration, the most sensual kiss I could deliver.

"Elijah," Hannah gasped when she finally parted from my lips.

"What is it, beauty?"

The gorgeous woman scrambled to sit up, pushing me back a bit too. "Jesus. You're trying to kill me with your mouth."

"Baby"—I kissed her mouth off center to the right—"if that were the case"—then kissed off center to the left—"my face would be between your legs." Before finishing my thought, when she expected I'd deliver a kiss full on her mouth, I sank my teeth into her bottom lip and tugged roughly on the juicy pad before letting go and whispering right against her abused cushions, "And only if you asked nicely."

She squeaked—actually whimpered—when I surprised her by kissing her so aggressively, she tumbled backward to lie flat again.

I was on her in a flash, grinding my rock-hard cock into her belly in long thrusts as though I were inside her.

I needed to be inside her.

"Take these fucking pants off. Now."

Her eyes popped open, and I don't know if it was my tone or the words that had her moving so quickly, but she knew I meant business, and she wasn't about to test me. Plus, I was really getting to know this girl's tells, and she was as horned up as I was.

Her eyes were glassy like she had a fever, and her cheeks were flushed red like it too. Hannah's body was as expressive as her mind, so there was just no hiding what she was feeling when her emotions were so intense.

"But we can't ... I mean ... not right here."

"The hell we can't." I pushed the empty food containers and magazines off the surface of the coffee table and met Hannah's disbelieving stare. "Right here, baby."

"What do you mean, right here?"

"Get your ass right here. Now."

"You can't be ser—"

I took her hand and tugged her so forcefully toward me, she tumbled into my arms. "Perfect," I said, hoisting her off the ground with my hands beneath her ass cheeks. "Wrap your legs around me."

After she did, I knelt down in front of the table while still holding her face-to-face. With the table right behind her now, she just had to disengage from the death grip she had around me and lie flat on the table, and she'd be like a sacrifice on my living room altar. Now that her jeans were off, I could see there were black lace panties that matched her bra. Lavender satin ribbon connected the front and back triangles of delicate fabric.

"Jesus Christ, Hannah."

She picked her head up to see what I was doing. She got an eyeful, all right.

My own pants were midthigh, and I gripped my dick, trying to regain some control over the situation before I erupted.

Even though her stare was fixed on my fist, she muttered, "What's wrong?"

"Nothing. You're so fucking hot. This black lace on your milky skin is making me crazy. I want to fuck you right through it."

"Uuhhh...oh...okay... Is that possible?" She shot her gaze up to meet mine. "Can you do that?"

I couldn't hold back my laugh at her innocent curiosity. "Anything's possible if you want it bad enough. We just need to make a hole for my cock. So they would be ruined." I shrugged, thinking of the image and the incredible fantasy that created in my mind. "Might be worth it."

"You're a madman!"

"When it comes to this pussy, I am." I ran a teasing fingertip along the edge of her black lace panties. First around the top edge at the waistband, then around each leg, taking extra care on the inside edge near her damp heat.

"Oh shit, Elijah. You're making me crazy with the teasing."

"Easy, now," I chastised. "What have I told you?"

"I know, I know!" she whimpered. "But it feels so good!"

"Tell me."

"I trust you with my pleasure. You'll always make it good for me."

"That's right. Is whining and being impatient you trusting me?"

"No. But—" Her protest came to a halt when I leaned in and fanned my warm breath across her sensitive flesh. A husky moan came from her throat instead.

I pulled her panties to the side and took a slow swipe across her swollen clit. Repeating the motion, back and forth, then sucking all her juicy pink folds into my mouth to savor every bit of her arousal. The taste, the smell, the feel—would never be enough. If I could crawl inside her and experience her from the inside out, it still wouldn't be enough.

Yeah, I was officially gone for this one. Long, long gone. The craziest part about that admission? I didn't want to be found. It felt just right where I was.

"Need to be inside." I choked off the sentence when Hannah stretched her arms above her head, arching her back and creating a sexy offering before me.

"I need that too," she said. "Please, right now."

"I won't come inside. I just need to feel you. Then I'll

stop. Just need to feel you." I didn't know who I was trying to convince with all the declarations, but I was quickly losing my mind with need.

"God, yes." She moaned and reached for me with both hands.

It was unlike both of us to get caught up in our lust so deeply that one of us didn't keep a partially sane mind, but I lined up at her entrance and started working my way inside her an inch or two before she gripped my arm with fierce strength and hissed, "Oh shit, yes. God, that feels good. Elijah, stop."

Wait. What?

"Stop?" I repeated.

"You don't have a condom?" she asked between pants.

"Not on me, no. I didn't expect to need one during dinner tonight. I'll go get one . . ."

"No. No, I'm sure it will be fine. Just this one time."

We were both old enough and wise enough to know better, but when caught in the heat of the moment and hormones were clouding all good sense and judgment, the words *just this one time* seemed perfectly reasonable.

So I pushed into her deeper. I let her body erase any coherent thoughts and drown in the rapture of lust that swirled around us while we fucked. With Hannah spread out on the coffee table, her body was positioned at the perfect height to hit all the best places inside her channel. Based on the possessed noises coming from my sexy goddess, she either agreed or had seen a demon and was trying to drive the thing off with the decibels of her own voice.

"Feel good, beauty? You like the way I fuck you, don't you?"

Hannah whimpered a reply between gasps.

"Answer me, baby. Feel good?"

"Yes! My God, yes! I don't know what's happening. It feels so good, it's freaking me out. I think I'm going to burst from here." She pushed the palm of her hand into her abdomen, very low near her pubic bone.

"That's a good girl. You're always so in tune with your body. Can you squeeze me from there? Flex those muscles you're pushing on." I stilled my movement while buried deep inside her and watched her face while she tried to figure out how to engage the muscles there. When she looked at me with a frustrated expression, I kissed her nose quickly and promised with a wink, "We'll keep practicing. You'll figure it out."

Then I covered her mouth with a more sensual kiss. All the squeezing and fluttering of her insides against my hard shaft had my eyes crossing with the need to release. I could already feel how close I was, and I swore to myself it wasn't going to happen inside her.

"I'm going to come all over these pretty panties, baby. I'm too close to hold it back."

"Do it. Let me watch you," Hannah said in that alto voice that stroked my dick as well as if she used her hands.

I pulled out, and she pushed to sit up and have a better view of what I was doing to myself, pumping my cock with my fist in a tight grasp to simulate the pressure of her cunt. A handful of short, tight tugs, and my balls drew up closer to my body.

Hannah made some sort of appraising hum, and I was gone. Hot spurts of come shot from the end of my cock and landed where I aimed on her lacy panties. For some depraved reason, the sight made my orgasm pulse on and on. Something about making my pure beauty dirty and naughty like me thrilled me to the core. A groan so low and feral sneaked out and blanketed the room.

I was still hard for this woman and really wanted to satisfy her too. After kissing her quickly, I rearranged her with her arms stretched across the table and her chest and belly flat on the top surface. I got behind her and slicked the head of my shaft through her wetness before sliding back in.

"Holy shit. My God. My God, Elijah. So good."

This position was usually a little harder for women to handle because of my anatomy, but we'd been fucking for a couple of months now, and although she'd never get completely comfortable with it, we both knew what her limits were. Typically, as long as I took it slow going in the first few strokes, she relaxed enough to enjoy the full experience, no matter what position we were in.

I gathered a fistful of Hannah's hair and cranked her head back until I could see her wild eyes.

"You like that? When I pull your pretty hair?"

She whimpered and closed her eyes, and I could only guess she was embarrassed to admit she liked playing a little rough. My God, if she only knew how rough things could get.

"Answer me, girl, so I know if it's yes or no." I pulled a little tighter on her hair in my fist.

"Ye-Yes. I like it. A lot," she said between exhales.

"Thank you. Is it the pain or the possession you like? I'm happy to give you more of either. Or both."

"I don't know. I don't know which it is. I haven't... this isn't..." She trailed off when she couldn't organize her thoughts.

"That's okay, baby. We'll figure it out together. And we'll have tons of fun doing so. But right now I need you to come for me. Are you close? Do you need me to push you over?"

She didn't scoff or question the offer. She knew I would make good on the proposal with a few minor adjustments. We'd been down that road before, and she knew I could play her body like a master.

"I'm close. It all feels so good. It always feels so good with you," Hannah whispered.

I tucked my forearm across her stomach and sat back on my heels, dragging her back with me so now she was basically sitting on my lap, albeit with a big, hard dick inside her.

"Oh, shit! Oh my God! Elijah!"

"You're in control now, beautiful. Ride me until you get what you need. Go." I pinched her ass, and she squawked.

When she rose up a few inches and air washed over the spot she had made contact, I was thrilled by how wet she was.

"Jesus Christ, girl. Your pussy is so hot and wet. Fuck, it feels so good on my lap when you sit all the way back." I grabbed her waist with both hands and held her against me, grinding up into her.

Hannah scrabbled at my fingers biting into the flesh at her midsection and said, "You said I was in control! Let go." She stared at me over her shoulder with challenge and . . . what else was this look? Command? Demand? So interesting, whatever it was. I would never have pegged her for a top, but I might have just stumbled onto something.

"Tell me where to put them. You tell me, and it's yours." I showed her both hands, palms facing her, fingers spread wide. I wasn't above taking direction from a woman if it fed her needs.

I saw the moment the fire lit inside her. From a spark to a flame, her desire blazed red-hot.

Oh shit, this is going to be fun now.

"Under me," she said. When I tilted my head a bit, trying to understand what she meant, she continued. "Under my ass. When I rise up, you touch anywhere and everywhere you can. Like you can't get enough. When I come down, you stay flat between us, like a layer cake. Your thighs, your flat hands, my ass. Got it?"

"I do. Go, move, girl." I'd probably have to draw the line at calling her ma'am. At least right now. Maybe I could work into it, but this was already so unfamiliar but wickedly hot. And seeing the gleam in her eyes, fuck me! My cock felt like I could explode any second.

But shit. I still didn't have a condom on.

"Babe," I tried to speak up, but she was all but drunk with arousal. "Han," I said again.

"Elijah, move. Come on, please. I'm so ready."

"Beautiful, I feel how ready you are, trust me. I feel every single flutter inside your tight cunt like this. But baby, still no condom."

"I don't care. Please don't stop. It's fine. I'm sure it's fine. I'll beg if I have to."

So when she rose up, I did what she wanted—no, *demanded*—and groped and played with her everywhere I could manage, using the sounds she made as my guide.

She was especially expressive in her newfound power position, so I had a clear understanding of what was working for her and what was just all right.

"Fuck, Hannah, you're so hot. I can't stop picturing my cock in this sweet ass."

She swung her head back to look at me so fast it was almost comical.

"One day, baby, you'll beg me to fuck you here. You'll see,"

I taunted while running my thumb across the tight hole. There was so much wetness from her pussy, I slicked it around her asshole too and applied a little pressure over the entrance. I knew she would panic if I entered her there without discussing it first, but I wanted her to get used to me owning every inch of her body.

"Oh, my God. Shit, why—why does that feel good? I don't think that should feel good," she said, her eyes pleading with me for an answer she could reason with.

"That's your first mistake, my love. You're thinking when you should just be feeling. Take your brain out of the equation and let your body run free. I will keep you safe. I promise." I kissed her shoulder blade and then licked the skin there, making the spot very wet before sinking my teeth in for a sizable bite.

"Ride me, woman. If I take over again, it's going to be hard and fast, and you'll be limping out of this room when I'm done."

She dropped her chin to her chest but started moving again. I could tell she had a lazy grin on her lips by the way her cheeks were shaped. She liked to act like my filthy comments offended her, but they really thrilled her. The rush of moisture from her channel was an undisputable giveaway.

In just a few more beats, Hannah was chanting my name mixed with the Lord's and "yeses" and "pleases" and begging me not to stop.

My grin was as wide as it could be, thinking about the fact that she was the one doing all the work, so my not stopping was of no consequence.

My own orgasm slammed into me like a tidal wave. It wasn't that I didn't feel it coming on—*I mean, be serious*. Some sensations are unique to only one result, and coming happens to be one of them.

Feeling Hannah's orgasm build, crest, and recede all from the deepest place inside her with the most sensitive part of my own body was equal parts heaven and torture. I was so wrapped up in her experience that the transference of pleasure was only natural. Forgetting for the umpteenth time that I wasn't wearing a condom should not have been. Being so careless with the potential of creating another life should not have been.

Pulling out at the final moment—and fine, maybe it was actually a moment too late—left warm, thick threads of milky white semen on her lower back as I strangled the last of my climax from my cock. There was no point in thrashing ourselves about the carelessness of what we'd just done, especially amid the discovery of my beautiful baby's dominant side.

Christ, was this going to be fun exploring with her. I couldn't remember the last time I let a woman top me. Or a dude for that matter. Probably the closest I'd come was a three-way with Bas, but that was a different dynamic all together.

After we both pulled our clothes back on, I crawled onto the sofa and nestled into my favorite corner spot. As I held my arms out, Hannah came to me and settled into the space in front of me, and we snuggled there for a while. I was so content inhaling the smell of her shampoo in her hair and sex on her skin. It was a heady combination, and my insatiable dick was twitching every time she moved her fine ass against me.

"Stop squirming or we're going again," I grumbled in a sleepy voice.

She giggled and thrust her curvy bottom back farther.

I dug my fingers into her hip and growled. "Do you think I'm joking?" I hooked my top leg over her so she could feel the unmistakable ridge of stiffness behind her.

"Jesus, man. Do you ever get enough?"

"With you? Apparently not."

"So you're not always like this?" she asked, and I wasn't sure if she really wanted to have this conversation or if she thought she was going to uncover something special that others hadn't.

"Like what?"

"Insatiable. Seriously, you have a really healthy sexual appetite, wouldn't you say?"

"I don't know. No more than any other healthy man my age. Especially tempted by a hot little seductress like you all the time. Are you complaining? I mean, you don't seem to be, between God's name and mine and those other creative things you yell about when you're coming!"

Hannah laughed and swatted at me without looking back, so she ended up swinging at empty air and looking ridiculous. We both laughed harder at her reaction.

Finally, she changed the subject. "What time is the rehearsal tomorrow?"

"I think they want us there at four. I have to look at the email to be sure."

"Do you want to fly with me in the morning? I have a scheduled launch at seven. I'll let you be on my ground crew if you're extra nice to me."

I dug my fingers into her ribs, and she squealed with laughter. "You're mighty sassy tonight. What's gotten into you?"

"You're an easy mark, Mr. Banks. I don't know what else to say."

"Oh, okay. That must be it." My comment was pure

sarcasm and accompanied by a teenager-styled eye roll so the point really drove home.

"But in all seriousness, let me check in with Grant and see if he has everything squared away for tomorrow night. As long as we don't have errands or anything to do for the bachelor party, I'm all yours until the rehearsal dinner."

"Good. I hope he has everything done, then. I love when you come along. It makes it so much better." She flipped over in the little bit of space she had on the sofa so we were nose to nose. "Do you know what?" she asked with a sheepish look.

"What?"

"You make everything I do better."

I gave her a slow, seductive kiss because that was one of the best things she'd ever said to me. Usually when I tried to talk seriously with her about my feelings, she quickly changed the subject or completely bolted from the room. Just up and walked away in a panic.

When we parted from the kiss, I said quietly, "Thank you for saying that."

"Thank you for being patient with me. For keeping me safe, and for all the things I don't even know about yet."

"You're very welcome, my beautiful queen. I'm a little confused about that last part, but—"

Hannah interrupted with, "I just know there are more things to come in the future that I don't know yet. So think of it as a preemptive thank-you."

"Well then, you're very welcome. One for now"—I gave her a lingering kiss—"and one for later." I followed that with another, longer, more intense kiss. When I finally released her, her blue eyes were wild and unfocused, and she had pink swatches high on her cheeks.

"My God, I feel like I hit the jackpot with you."

I couldn't help but laugh at that comment. I knew she meant it as a compliment, but it sounded like I was a prize steer at a county fair.

"I think I'm the winner here," I said against her lips.

CHAPTER TWO

HANNAH

"How long has she been in there?" my friend and boss, Rio Gibson, asked as she barged through the first set of doors into the master suite of Abbigail's hilltop Calabasas home.

I was perched outside the second set of doors that led into the bathroom portion of the expansive suite, while Abbi's personal assistant, Dori, was on the frontline with her boss lady and bride.

"Abs, you better blow and go, sister. He's on his way up here, and I think he's onto you this time, girl." Rio let the hem of her bridesmaid dress flutter to the ground so she could pound on the door while she shouted her warning. She gave me a skeptical look and shook her head, mouthing *she's so busted* just before pounding on the door again.

"Ab-i-gail Ei-leen!" Each syllable was punctuated by the woman's tiny fist on the door.

The door flew open just as Rio raised her fist to knock again, and I caught the little ball in my hand midstrike, or Dori would've been punched right in the face. Given their history, I wasn't sure Rio would've been too sorry about it, either.

After closing the door behind her in the calmest manner then standing in front of it like one of the Queen's very own Beefeaters, Dori asked, "Where is Mr. Shark right now?"

"He's on his way up here from the back lawn," Rio answered, still somewhat hysterical. "I saw him headed this way and ran up the back stairs."

"Okay, so let's all act natural. He's not allowed to see his bride before she walks down the aisle, so I'll head him off outside this door."

"Oh! Like that's going to work." Rio scoffed. "Have you tried telling that man no? About anything?"

I felt like I was watching a tennis match the way these two were volleying back and forth.

"It will be fine. He's a big kitten beneath all that bluster. You'll see. As long as everyone just acts natural."

Dori gave herself an approving nod and said, "That's when he gets agitated. When he senses something is off. He truly is like his namesake."

It was a good thing at least *she* had faith in her plan. Rio and I weren't as convinced.

"Ohhhh, Dori. Dooorrii, Doorrrii, Dori." Rio said her name over and over in a singsong voice, just patronizing the woman.

Meanwhile, Abbi's assistant looked like she was about to throat punch my little boss.

"Rio?" Abbi called in the smallest voice I think I'd ever heard from her, and Rio stopped antagonizing Dori and rushed to the bathroom, where Abbi was peeking through a sliver of open space.

"What, Mama? What can I do for you? Besides give your lady-in-waiting the loose change in my pocketbook so she can buy a clue?"

I had to stifle my own laughter at that one. I had to hand it to this little spitfire. Through all the crap that life had thrown in this woman's path, she still had a spunky little attitude and a funny-as-hell sense of humor. I would love to go out with her and my sister Agatha sometime. I think my sides would be sore from laughing so much by the end of the night with those two in the same place.

"Can you go down the hall to the game room? There's a fridge in there. Please get me some sort of clear soda. Ginger ale or Sprite or something like that? I'm hoping like hell this is just nerves and will go away."

Rio tilted her head to the side while Abbi spoke, basically calling her on her shit, but Abbi just put her hand out.

"I know, I know. But it's too early to take a test, and my period isn't even late yet. Not for two weeks. There's no point speculating until we have some way to prove it," Abbigail protested, and I had to admit, she made a lot of sense.

"Were you guys trying?" I asked from my post at the door.

"Well, we weren't *not* trying, if that makes sense."

Of course that made me think of the two times Elijah and I had had unprotected sex in the past forty-eight hours. I wondered what his reaction would be if I told him I was late. Would he be over the moon or lose his shit? Was he ready to be a father?

It was probably too soon for the two of us to make that sort of commitment to each other, although I felt like I could with him. I didn't feel like I needed to sleep around with fifty different men to know I'd landed the perfect one.

I had come to a decision last night, though, while I lay awake staring at the ceiling. I'd watched the trees outside the windows make shadows on the nighttime ceiling above my head and come to a realization. It was based on an old saying that a man would never buy a cow if he were getting his milk for free. With our current arrangement, Elijah was not only getting the milk for free, but he also had the full service. Creamer, butter, yogurt, ice cream, cheese—basically anything you could find in the dairy section of the grocery store—right at his fingertips.

I needed to go home. I needed to move out of Elijah's house and back to my own. It would be hard to adjust to and I would miss him terribly, but I would like to see him put in some effort to obtain his dairy products instead of the current home delivery service he was subscribed to.

Maybe it was old-fashioned of me to think that way, but I didn't have anything else to go on. It was the way I was raised. Hell, my parents still didn't know I was living with a man, nor had they met him. But that wasn't Elijah's fault. He'd tried to force the opportunity on a few occasions, but for whatever reason, I'd done everything in my power to thwart the plan.

I couldn't figure out what I feared so much. Probably that my mom would fall in love with him instantly. He was so handsome and debonair. The man oozed charm and servility— basically everything a mother would want in a partner for her daughter.

My dad would be impressed by his intelligence and confidence. Elijah had a particular bearing when he entered a room. It instantly let everyone else know *don't fuck with me*, but he was still completely approachable and friendly. It was a combination few were able to pull off. With my guy—and yes, I called him mine all the time in my mind—it just came naturally. The demeanor was authentic, and whoever was around him sensed that, so he was liked and trusted by everyone. Elijah Banks was an all-around good man. Both my mom and dad would encourage me to hold on with both hands.

When my sisters met this guy, they would go crazy. He was so good-looking, and more than likely, at least one of them would embarrass me and say something completely inappropriate or tell him some ridiculous childhood story that no date should ever be exposed to. That was exactly why they would do it, too! Siblings had that special privilege to taunt and tease you in those merciless ways no one else got to, and you still loved them at the end of the day. Of course, you were also plotting their demise while hugging them and telling them you didn't hold a grudge, but that was the best part of it all. Paybacks were indeed a bitch.

Pounding on the bedroom door shook me from my musings, and we all looked at each other with wide eyes.

Dori sprang into action and went to answer the caller, but we already knew who it was because he was shouting the moment his fist left the wood panel.

"Abbigail. Open this door."

You could hear the knob rattle as he tried to get through the locked portal.

Dori swung the door wide just as Sebastian Shark raised his fist to pound again. She reared back to narrowly miss getting punched for the second time today. The poor woman was going to need to collect hazardous duty pay working in this house.

"Hey there, Mr. Groom. Shouldn't you be downstairs greeting guests?"

"I wanted to make sure my wife-to-be is all right," he insisted as Dori drove him from the doorway with both hands on the center of his broad chest.

Holy hell, she was actually touching him. From everything I understood from Elijah, that was a major no-go in the Shark universe.

"She's fine," Dori responded in a gentle voice as she hooked her foot around the bottom of the door to swing the thing shut, effectively closing them out into the hall.

Damn, the girl was good. No denying that.

"Hannah? Are you still out there?" Abbi's quiet whisper came from behind the bathroom door.

I gathered up the skirt of my bridesmaid's dress and hustled over to the locked door. "Yeah, what's up?"

"Has Rio come back with the drink?"

"No, and now Mr. Shark is out in the hall, so hopefully she will take a detour or remain out of sight until he goes back downstairs."

"That's what I was thinking too. If he sees what she has, it will be a dead giveaway. I lived on ginger ale, tea, and toast with Kaisan."

"Why not just tell him?" I asked. Maybe there was something I was missing, but wouldn't he be happy?

"Because he will make me lie in bed for the next nine months again, and I'm not doing that. I almost went crazy last time."

"But weren't you in danger or something?"

"Yeah, a danger that hasn't been fully handled. We still don't know who kidnapped Grant or if it had anything to do with all the crazy stuff that happened here and to Bas. And of course, my brother . . ."

Shit. Damn it.

I should've kept my mouth shut. It made sense why no one was bringing up what I just had. All roads led back to that one really crappy detail. Abbi's brother—Rio's late husband— was dead, and it probably had something to do with Sebastian

Shark. If you asked Rio to tell the story, there was no *probably* about it.

Dori and Rio came back into the bedroom together. Rio had a small bottle of Sprite in one hand and a can of ginger ale in the other hand. Dori looked like she'd been on the front line of a skirmish and had taken a bullet or two and lost some blood.

I couldn't help but chuckle when I asked, "Are you okay?"

"Jesus, that man can be difficult. He's so stubborn. I see where that baby gets it from."

Abbigail finally came swishing out of the bathroom and sat carefully on the edge of the bed. "Are you really just figuring that out now?"

"Talk about a dog with a bone." Dori shook her head in disbelief.

"Our son is a chip off that block for sure. We joked about it when I was pregnant and so sick that he was going to have Sebastian's temperament because he was already giving me such a hard time, but I don't think either of us had a clue what we were really in for." Abbi laughed and looked wistful as she remembered.

"Let me call the makeup girl in so we can get you finished and down there on time, or he's going to be up here again. I'm sure of it." The thought of Mr. Shark returning had Dori going pale again as she held her cell phone to her ear, waiting to connect to the cosmetologist.

"Where is she that you have to call her?" I asked while she waited.

"I told her to go eat something—that it would probably be a long day. You know, pictures and everything." Dori quickly turned her back and started speaking to the person on the other end of the line when the call connected, abruptly ending our side conversation.

Finding Rio's gaze halfway across the room, I asked, "So are you taking notes? You ready to do this?"

"I don't know if we'll go through all this." She waved her hand through the air to encapsulate the whole wedding pageantry. "Since I've done it once before and Grant isn't really this kind of guy and doesn't have family, I think we'll sneak off to Vegas or something."

Abbi chimed in, "I hope you invite us, at least. I mean the four of us." She motioned to me and back to herself, and of course meant our guys too.

"I can barely picture one of them taking a piss without the other two there, let alone getting married." Rio rolled her eyes and chuckled. "So yeah, I just assumed you guys would be there too."

"Wait," I said to Abbi with the most serious tone I could manage, even though I was completely joking. "I thought we were going on your honeymoon with you." The best jokes were the ones told with a straight face. "Have you found out where we're going yet so I can pack accordingly?" I made quick eye contact with Rio and winked while Abbi fussed with the length of her slip.

When she looked up, Abbi shifted her stare from me to Rio. She looked so uncomfortable, I almost burst out laughing. Poor thing. But Rio kept the gag going a bit longer.

"Oh, thanks for reminding me, Hannah. I meant to ask about that earlier. I need to set up the sitter for Robert, and the girl I like can be hard to get in a pinch. How many days are we going for, exactly? Do we know?"

Now we both stared at Abbigail, one of us on either side of her, so no matter which way she turned, she got an eyeful of a friend's expectant stare. Until, of course, Dori walked back into the room and blew the whole thing.

"What's going on?" The assistant bounced her gaze from the bride to me, back to Abbi, then Rio before demanding, "Why do you look like you've seen a ghost? What did I miss? Was he in here again? I'm going to hang that man up by his—"

Rio and I burst out laughing—no, more like cackling at that point—because the combined looks on Abbigail's and Dori's faces were so priceless. I really was kicking myself for not having my phone at the ready.

"You are so fucking evil!" Abbi shouted and launched herself at Rio.

Rio put her spindly arms up in front of her face to try to protect herself from the bride on a rampage, but we were all laughing so hard, no actual harm was caused.

Dori, the forever wet towel, stood back with her hands on her hips and *tsk*ed.

"You're going to ruin your hair," she chastised. "Abbigail, really!"

"Dori!" we all yelled in unison.

"Shut up, will ya?" Rio voiced what I was thinking.

★ ★ ★

Abbigail and Sebastian became mister and missus that afternoon as the sun set over the Pacific Ocean. They had a small crowd at their home to celebrate the occasion, and other than Abbi's periodic dashes to the bathroom, everything seemed perfect.

By midnight, I was exhausted, and Elijah must have seen me yawn one too many times because strong arms came from behind to cradle me in the safest, warmest embrace as I stood talking to Rio and Grant.

"Are you ready to go?" my sexy landlord rumbled in my ear.

"Whenever you are. I don't want to drag you away from the party before you're ready."

"I would've left after the sun went down if it meant we were going home to do our own thing," he growled for only me to hear.

"Is that right?" I teased and turned in the circle of his arms and linked my hands at his nape. "I had a lovely time here with you tonight. Thank you for being my date."

"Beautiful girl, I will be your date anywhere and everywhere you'll have me."

"Oh, you're full of all the right lines tonight I see."

He gave me a playful wink and dipped me back with a kiss so deep and passionate, I wasn't sure if the stars I saw were from the change in position or the arousal flooding my body. When we stood upright again, I fluttered my hand up to my chest, where I could feel my heart beating wildly, and then chased the heat up my neck and to my cheek, where I was sure I must have been fire engine red.

"My God, you are a vision when you're aroused," Elijah said.

I was lost in his icy green eyes that looked positively magical in the flickering lights strung from every possible place inside the giant tent the Sharks had set up for the party.

"Keep that up, Mr. Banks, and we won't make it out of the car." I grabbed his hand and playfully tugged him toward the exit of the reception.

"I like the way you're thinking! I'll tell Lorenzo to take the long way home."

"Let's make a lap and say our goodbyes first. Before you get any wild ideas."

Elijah let his shoulders drop dramatically like a boy who just had his toys taken away, and I burst out laughing.

Two couples we were passing stopped midconversation and turned to see what was so funny.

He widened his eyes at me playfully. "See what you've done?"

"Me?" I laughed again. "You're the one acting like a child."

"I don't know, young lady. I think punishments are in order."

"Oh, don't even try it." I pushed his shoulder, and he overreacted and threw his body off center.

"Hey. Watch it, lady."

"Oh my God." I covered my mouth, laughing in such a fit I had to stop walking. "You're acting crazy. I think I better get a ride from someone else. Getting into a car with you might be hazardous to my health."

Quickly, he grabbed me around the waist and hauled me against him. Our bodies crashed together so forcefully, I made a *hmmpphh* sound when I smacked into him.

"You'll do no such thing. Ever again," he said in a lethally calm and frighteningly seductive tone.

And my God . . . The sizzling look he gave me along with the threat could've lit me on fire, it was so damn hot. My throat went instantly dry.

Shit.

"Uhhh—okay. You knooooow . . ." I drew the word out and leaned back from his embrace so I could drag my index finger down his sternum. "You're pretty sexy when you get all bossy like that. Has anyone ever told you that?"

He tick-tocked his head back and forth, his hair flopping from one side to the other with his movement. My panties turned to ashes on the spot. *Poof.* Just up in flames from the smoldering look this man gave me.

Shit.

I was in for the ride of my life. If not the car, then the moment we got home. I could smell the sex coming off him in waves by the time we got out to the driveway. Lorenzo opened the back door of the limousine, and I scampered in first.

Elijah groaned when he had a view of my backside, and I couldn't hear what he was telling Lorenzo, but they chuckled with each other, and my landlord gave the other man a hearty thump on the back before getting in the back seat with me.

The privacy divider was already engaged, so the moment the door closed, it was very dark and very quiet in our portion of the vehicle.

"Wow, what a wonderful evening. I'm so tired though, aren't you?" I made a big show of yawning and stretching and snuggling into his side like I was going to sleep the whole way home. "Actually, would you mind if I put my head in your lap?" I asked with the widest, most innocent eyes I could manage. Inside, I was thinking this wouldn't last more than two minutes before he was squirming beneath me.

"No, baby. If you'd be more comfortable, I'm all yours."

"Thank you." I lay across the seat and burrowed my face into his lap, using my hands as a makeshift pillow. "Are you sure you don't mind?"

"Totally fine," Elijah said, his voice low in his chest. "Would your hair feel better down? I'm going to take all these pins out for you while you lie there. It will give me something to focus on other than your face a centimeter from my dick."

"I thought something felt a little firm in here," I said and gave him a squeeze.

"Hannah. Rochelle. This is the only warning I'm going to give you."

"Okay, okay. I'll be good."

"I know you'd be good. That's the problem I'm having at the moment. Be quiet and go to sleep."

"Okay. Night, Mr. Banks."

"Night, beauty."

One by one, he plucked the bobby pins from the complicated up-do my hair was styled in. Because there was so much of it, it took no less than thirty of those little buggers to hold my hair in place. Finally, as he massaged my head, his fingers made their way through to my scalp without encountering any pins.

"My God, that feels sooooo good. Mmmm."

"Stop. Brat," he muttered.

"What?" I tried to sound innocent with my query.

"Nice try. You know exactly what you're doing. Don't think you're not going to pay for this torture you're putting me through the very second we get into my room. I think it's time I show you all the rig points on that bedframe."

"Rig points?" I gulped. "Are you talking about places to tie things down?"

"Not things, beautiful. People. Or person in this case— namely you. I wish it were lighter in here so I could see your reaction right now. Instead, I'll have to rely on your words. Tell me what you think of that idea," Elijah purred in the most seductive voice. "Be specific."

"Ummm..."

"Have you been restrained before? During sex, I

mean?" he asked, stroking his strong fingers from the ball of my shoulder up the length of my bare neck. "You looked completely breathtaking today. Did I tell you that?" Now his voice vibrated through his body because it had dipped into a register so low.

Shivers snaked along my spine and up into my hairline, chasing his fingertips that wound through my tresses.

"You may have mentioned it." I smiled into his thigh when I answered. If he kept up the tender touches to that sensitive skin though, I might sink my teeth into the leg I was using for a pillow.

"Answer my question, Ms. Farsey."

"Mmmm, that feels so nice," I murmured. "No," I answered using an equally quiet voice.

"No you won't answer me, or no you've never been bound by a lover?"

"The second one," I said in a rush. I was so awkward when it came to talking about this stuff, and he knew it. Elijah, on the other hand, could talk about stock dividends in one sentence and butt plugs in the next and never change the cadence of his delivery.

"Do you trust me enough to let me tie you to my bed, Hannah? Can I bind you?" He lifted my arm to lay along my ear, so I looked like a dancer stretching her torso at the barre while warming up. The man was so smooth, though, because he knew exactly what he would find beneath that arm. Straightaway, he began tugging down the zipper to my gown.

Slowly—so slowly—my God, I swore I could hear each individual tooth move through the pull as he lowered the zipper one inch then another. His seduction was so sinful, so perfect, a moan clawed up my throat, and I had to keep my lips pressed tightly together so the needy sound wouldn't run free. I was already so aroused, my panting breaths were bouncing around the car's interior like a drumbeat in a racquetball court.

"Look at these beautiful tits," he said in what sounded like fascination. "There isn't an inch of this body that isn't perfect, do you know that?" Elijah drew my zipper down another inch while he caressed the exposed skin.

But then he froze and took a deep breath.

When I went to sit up, thinking surely he must've seen something out the window or forgotten something back at the Sharks' house, he held me in place where I lay across his lap.

"What is it? What's wrong?"

"Nothing's wrong, gorgeous girl. Not a damn thing."

"Well, you kind of startled for a moment. It was like you thought of something, maybe?"

"You're so smart. Smart and stunning. I'm the luckiest fucker alive. Don't think I don't realize it, Hannah."

"So what's going on?"

He started tugging my zipper back up, righting my dress so I would be decent to exit the car, I presumed.

"I just made a decision. A very important one."

"Ohhhhkay. Are you going to let me in on this decision? Does it involve me?" Why was this like pulling teeth all of a sudden? He loved toying with me in every way. Building the intention of the moment.

"Of course it does. Everything I do, everything I say—hell, every breath I take these days—is with you in mind."

Oh boy. I wasn't sure I liked the sound of all that. Especially since I had planned on moving back to my parents' home in the morning. That didn't sound like he was going to make it an easy departure.

"Tell me!" I said impatiently while I sat up fully and looked down to make sure the girls were tucked into the bodice of my dress and I looked fairly put together.

"Tonight, I'm claiming you as mine," Elijah said resolutely.

"What?"

"Which part did you not understand?"

"Well, the whole caveman thing was a little antediluvian, no?"

"No. I want the world to know we're together. I want it to be official. When the sun comes up tomorrow, everyone will know who you belong to. Me. Mine."

He leaned over to where I sat, staring at him as if he'd sprouted a set of antlers and maybe a tail, and gave me a kiss so forceful, I saw stars dance behind my eyelids.

CHAPTER THREE

ELIJAH

Well, that might have been a bit much. If I were judging solely on the expression frozen on my girl's face, then I would have to say without a doubt, it was more truth than she was ready to hear.

But in her typical style, she gave her head an almost imperceptible shake—barely visible—and if not for Lorenzo opening the limo's door on her side first, I might have actually missed it. No such luck for her, though. I saw the reboot. Hannah cleared the cobwebs, plastered on her fake good nature, and thanked our driver with a brightness that could rival the noontime summer sun.

The man made eye contact with me from behind her as he shuffled along in her wake to where I already stood, waiting for my goddess to go inside for the night.

"Lorenzo, my man," I said and gave him a friendly handshake, leaning in for a pat on the back as well. "Thank you for bringing us home. We'll be in for the night. See you tomorrow?"

"I'm off for the next few days, actually. Heading up the coast to Napa for some personal time."

"Ahhh, that's right. I remember when you were first making those plans. Well, I hope that bed-and-breakfast is exactly what you were looking for. Enjoy your time away."

"Thank you, Mr. Banks. And thank you again for calling ahead to make the reservations. That was so kind of you." My driver shuffled his feet, still uncomfortable with my generosity after all these years.

"It was my pleasure. It was the least I could do. We'll see you in a few days."

With that, Hannah scooped up my hand, and we went through the front gate and up the curved, pebble-covered sidewalk to the front door. I pulled out my phone and used the home security app to turn off the alarm and open the front door.

"After you, my queen," I said, pushing the door open wide for Hannah to go in before me. A strategic pathway of lights came on when the front door was disengaged via the same app, so we could easily and safely find our way through the house to the master bedroom.

I had a very strong desire to whisk Hannah into my arms and carry her to my bed, where I planned to ravish her until the sun came up.

So that was exactly what I did. With her hand still clutched in mine, I pulled her body to my chest, bent low, and swept her legs right out from beneath her. The fantastic white-and-gold dress she wore had a full, floor-length skirt, so estimating where the bends of her knees were within all that fabric was close to rocket science. Luckily, I guessed quite accurately, and when she folded her legs over my arm, I was able to readjust and get a better grip.

Hannah laughed, wrapped her arms around my neck, and looked into my eyes. "What are you doing, crazy man?"

"I told you in the car." I let the quiet settle between us as I rounded the corner into the master suite. "Making you mine."

"Elijah." She breathed my name more than spoke it.

Whatever part of my heart wasn't already aching for this woman finally broke free from where I had been guarding it and keeping it safe for all these years. That damn throbbing organ tried to make a break for it by way of my throat, based on the size of the lump choking off my air supply. It was as though the vital muscle knew it would be safer in her keeping than anywhere else. Certainly than if I were to continue guarding it.

Officially she had all of me. Because with her, my heart could right itself. Mend its weary pieces and thrive again—be whole again. And in exchange, I'd give her all of me. My whole body. My whole mind. My whole soul too, if I even had such a thing—and more importantly, if she even wanted those things.

I thought I would never say any of this regarding a woman again as long as I lived. But I wanted to pledge it all to Hannah Rochelle Farsey. Because she was the kindest, smartest, most beautiful woman I had ever laid eyes on.

With tender kisses to her lips, nose, cheeks, and eyes, I situated her in the center of my bed. I backed off to stand and look down at her. My perfect queen. A goddess for this mortal man. And how did I get so lucky? How did I get to be the fool she came to and trusted that day with her safety?

It gave me chills thinking I'd forever be in Rio Gibson's debt for this miracle in the middle of my king-size mattress. But every win had a price. All in all, being grateful to Grant's little lady was a minor debt to pay.

"Baby, I'm going to make you feel so good tonight, you're going to forget your name," I vowed before covering her mouth with mine as my hunger for her flesh grew. "First, though, I want you out of this dress and tethered to my altar."

"Your altar? Oh my goodness." She grinned. "You are full of it tonight, aren't you?"

"I'm telling you, I'm going to worship this perfect body. And beauty, while I'm down on my knees, I'll be giving thanks to whoever the fuck brought you into my life. You have made every day worth waking up for. Lift your arm for me, love."

Hannah did as I asked while she writhed on my bed in the white garter belt and nude thigh-high stockings I'd given her this morning. I'd left the package for her in Abbi's room, where the women were getting ready, and she had whispered how much she loved it the first chance she had. She'd even gotten daring enough to steal me away to one of the guest bathrooms of the Shark house during the reception to let me sneak a peek. My dick had throbbed every time I'd thought about it since.

God, how times had changed. I'd fucked so many women in bathrooms like that. Women who happily stole me away during a wedding reception or other fancy affairs and had gotten on their knees to thank me in a more creative way for a gift so thoughtful and sexy.

Maybe they'd let me hike up their pretty dress and bend them over the vanity, and we'd both watch in the mirror while I showed her how much I liked the way the garters slipped and slid back and forth on her tight ass and thighs with every thrust of my hips.

Oh, but not Hannah. No, not her.

Because this girl was a class act. She was the purity my soul needed to get through this dark, dirty world. She was the light that would guide me home every night. Goodness when I had blanketed myself with a life of depravity for so long, her clean aura stung my eyes to view and burned my lungs when I inhaled.

"Don't move. I want to get a few things." I kissed her quickly and backed away from the bed, watching to see if she would obey. Immediately, she made to sit up, just like I suspected she would, until she found my icy stare fixed on her.

"I don't think you even considered trying to do what I asked," I reprimanded, voice quiet but husky and threatening all at the same time. My erection bobbed heavy in front of me when I dropped my tuxedo pants and boxers.

"Oh, man," she said, staring as if she hadn't seen me naked two hundred times before.

"Han?"

She snapped her mouth closed and lifted her eyes to find mine.

"Do. Not. Move."

"Ooohh kaaaay. But what's the big deal if I move?"

This curious kitten, always asking why instead of just obeying.

"You have a terrible time doing what you're told, and I'm worried you're going to find yourself in a bad situation because of it. I tell you things all the time for your own safety, but how can I trust you are doing them when you won't even sit still in the middle of the bed when I ask you to?"

"But Eli—"

If I had to place a bet right then, I would've said she was going to reach for the throw on the foot of the bed to cover herself while we spoke. Shield herself. She probably felt vulnerable sitting there, mostly naked, while I lectured her.

Her indigo eyes darted to the foot of the bed, and then she inched her foot down toward the fake fur blanket strewn artfully across the coverlet. Deciding to let her have the rope to hang herself with, I kept quiet and ducked into my closet to grab some gear to tie her to the bed for the night and a ball gag I was sure she would freak out about, simply because it would be punishment in its own right.

Back at the bedside, I dropped the cuffs and gag beside her hip and watched her take it all in.

"What is all that?"

"More gifts for you, beautiful. What do you think? Want to try them on?"

"Ummm, I don't know, Elijah," she said skeptically. Nervously. "Do I have to?"

"No. Of course not," I answered with the most carefree spirit I could slide into place. "You never have to do anything you don't want to do. But check this out…" I nudged my way onto the mattress beside her hip and sat with a bent leg under my ass. I held out my hands, flat palms up, hoping she would have faith and give me hers too.

"Good," I said with great appreciation when she did. "Now…" I exhaled and stared into her twinkling eyes. She was as excited as she was apprehensive. Which one begot the other, I wondered. "You trust me. Yes?"

"Of course I do," she breathed her relieved answer.

"Because I've never hurt you or betrayed you."

"I know."

"Nor will I ever," I vowed, and it wasn't sweet talk to get in the girl's knickers. It was a solemn oath. My complete truth.

"I believe you."

"Good, baby. I'm glad you understand how serious I am about the honesty in those words." I lifted her delicate but strong fingers to my lips and brushed them across my mouth over and over.

She stared at me the entire time, lips gently falling apart

to form a sweet little *O* while she watched.

"Here's the fun part of these gifts. I put these on your wrists"—I showed her the smaller set for her hands—"and this pair on your sexy ankles that I love so much."

The woman already knew I was obsessed with the insides of her ankles, so she gave me that shy smile. The one I told myself she saved just for me and times like this.

"There are eye hooks on the bed frame and straps that hook into these." I snagged my thumb in the ring on the cuff to demonstrate how the rigging worked. "Then you're mine to taunt and tease and bring pleasure to. God, Hannah . . ." I rolled my eyes back dramatically and then finished the thought. "So much pleasure you'll cry from it. Over and over again."

"Oh" was all she said at first, and really, it was more of a catch of sound when she sharply inhaled than an intentional response.

I tilted my head and waited, the motion enough to topple the longer section of my hair to the side to sweep over my forehead and part of my eye.

"Shit," she chuckled. "You are a lethal man cocktail, Elijah Banks. I'd be a fool to say no to what you're offering here. Right?"

"Far as I can tell." I shrugged and finger-combed my hair back into place.

"So what is the other thing? The dog collar and rubber ball?" my beauty asked.

"That's a ball gag. And we can use that if you get too loud or if you need correcting. Believe it or not, some people actually like them."

"You can't be serious."

"As a heart attack."

"Do you?"

"Do I what, beauty?"

"Do you like them?"

"That depends."

"On what? Be specific."

Ahhh, she'd finally caught on to my word game and raised the difficulty level a bit. "If you're asking if I would enjoy putting it on you or wearing it myself."

She turned her head slightly to the side and looked at me so suspiciously, I couldn't help but chuckle.

"What's that look?" I already had both wrist cuffs on and one ankle cuff. I was just finishing the second ankle when she answered. Having this conversation was the perfect distraction from what was going on right in front of her.

"I'm trying to imagine you with that ball"—she reached out, her arm a little heavier with the cuff and hardware in place, to stroke her index fingertip over the cleft of my upper lip, across the lip itself, and then as she dragged her nail over my bottom lip, finished her thought—"between your pouty lips." She swallowed roughly after she said it, and I was almost dizzy with how quickly my eyes darted from feature to feature of her face, throat, and chest, trying to catalog her arousal.

Her eyes were glazed and wide, and I'd bet next month's salary her pussy was wet. This girl was a natural switch, and I was surer of it every time one of these powerful moments happened between us.

I launched my full weight onto her and took her mouth so roughly, I knocked her onto her back. Climbing right over her, I stretched the entire length of her body and then pressed her into the mattress. I circled my hips into her cleft over and over while diving into her fathomless stare and feasting on her luscious mouth.

"You're picturing it and liking it, aren't you?" I taunted between drugging kisses.

"I-I-I don't know why—what it is about these things that you suggest?" She took a deep breath, then pointedly exhaled. "Seriously, Elijah, I feel like I just swam a five hundred, and all you did was suggest something perverted. What are you doing to me?"

"First of all, it's not perverted. If I like it, and you like it, we're both consenting adults. What we do in our house is our business."

"I know. I know all that. That was a poor word choice. My brain is scrambled. I-I-" she continued to stammer.

"My love," I began again and pushed up off her and then off the bed to attach her cuffs to the frame. "Let's not worry about it, and one day, we'll swap roles and see what you think of being the top. If it's not for you, then it's not for you." I lifted my shoulders and let them fall again. A careless shrug. It really was that simple.

I moved down to attach her feet while she gave her left hand a good yank and then repeated the motion with the right. Why did people always feel the need to do that? It had to be the same part of the brain that insisted on touching the plate no less than two seconds after the waitress says, *Careful, hon, this plate is hot, 'kay?*

Every. Damn. Time.

Prowling back to the woman of my fantasies, my dreams, my hopes, and desires, I mounted her once more. I gazed down to appreciate the innocence she'd managed to hold on to all these years. In the same world that made me the devil's imp that I was, she'd managed to remain so pure. I was in awe of her. In need of her. In love with her.

"Kiss me," Hannah said quietly. Seductively.

"Oh, sweetheart, I'm going to kiss every inch of this body, at least twice. I'm just coming up with a game plan here."

"Kiss me, please."

"All in good time. All in good time. That begging works for me, though. You can say *please* so prettily anytime you want. My cock sure likes it. Have you felt how hard I am for you?"

"Elijah," she whined then moaned, and I wasn't even touching her yet. "Please, touch me. Kiss me. I need you."

"I need you too, beautiful. So, so badly. How does it feel to have your legs spread open like that? No relief for that pretty pussy in that position, is there?"

"No," she whimpered, "there isn't."

"This lingerie is amazing on your skin. I knew it would be when I saw it." I ran my index finger under the straps that connected the garter belt to the hose before popping the clasp open. "Were you proud or embarrassed to receive a gift like this in front of your girlfriends? Proud that your man finds you so irresistible?" I gave the other side the same delicate, seductive treatment. "Proud that he thinks about this sexy, incredible body constantly?"

"Yes."

I just studied her, waiting for her to elaborate.

"I was very proud you'd been so thoughtful," she said with a sly grin.

"Oh, that smile has a story behind it, I think. What aren't you telling me? Did the girls tease you? Or did you all tease each other? Hmmm? Maybe you all helped Abbigail take the edge off before her big day?"

It took her about half a minute, but finally, Hannah figured out what I meant. "Elijah. Banks. No."

"So emphatic, beauty." My grin grew wider at her incredulous stare. "Are you saying you've never fooled around with a woman? I don't know, Farsey. You're full of surprises. I'll never presume to know something about you until you confirm or deny it with your own mouth."

"Well, I'm completely denying it. With my own mouth."

"But let's talk about that mouth," I said in a very low growl, already thinking about her lips wrapped around my cock and her tongue caressing the shaft on that sensitive spot she knew so expertly. She didn't have a ton of experience when I met her, true. But goddamn, the girl was a quick study.

Hannah looked up at me while I straddled her torso.

"You look like perfection right now. Utter perfection tethered to my bed. Now, I seem to recall promising to worship every inch of this body until you cried. Yes? What do you think? Are you ready, baby?"

"Honestly, you're scaring me a little bit. I don't think I've ever seen your eyes so dark. You look... I don't know? Sinister?"

"Is that right?"

She just nodded.

Next came a brazen combination that I could only hope would dazzle and daze her. With a far lean to the left to kiss her palm still shackled to the bed, I launched my first provocative interrogative.

"What one thing scares you most, Hannah Rochelle?" After my issuance, I continued making my way over her body's landscape with my greedy mouth. Every half inch or so, I would stop to nuzzle, kiss, lick, or bite her perfect flesh.

"Be honest now. Tonight, I want all your secrets. All you can bare."

"I can't … it's so hard … too hard …" Hannah whimpered.

"I know, baby. You should feel it firsthand. It's exquisite torture."

The woman leveraged that damn husky laugh like a weapon. But Christ, I was thrilled to see her engaging in my playful—well, for the most part—battle here and not just lying there and letting me steamroll right over her. Thinking these positive things about my woman gave me an idea of a little twist to add to my total truth game I was playing. Not only would I demand her answers, but I would reward her with some of my own as well.

"I was going to say it's too hard to think clearly when you're doing that. Oh, shit. Elijah! My Gooooood …"

"Do you want me to stop, then?" I gave her the tilted-head look, and she moaned.

"No. Please, no. It feels so good."

"I need your answer right now, or I will."

Hannah bucked against her bonds unexpectedly, and I was pretty sure if she hadn't been tethered to the headboard, she would've had both fists full of my hair holding me right where I was.

As if I needed encouragement.

"Abandonment," she moaned.

"Oh, baby, never. I promise with my entire heart." I went completely still and waited for her to make visual contact with me. "Never. Do you understand me?"

"I do," she whimpered and let her eyes drift closed. "I understand you." Then she whispered, "Please don't stop. Please."

"Mmmm. Sounds so pretty. I like this game. It's like a kinky truth or dare, but all truth. Let's see …" I hummed against her neck and then sucked the skin so hard she'd probably have a mark. Her moan was like an erotic standing ovation, so I moved a little lower and did it again. So fine, she'd have two marks.

Letting my voice dip down low, I said beside her ear, "Open your eyes and look at me, girl."

I became reacquainted with her azure stare now so heavy with sexual languor she could be the *It Girl* for a new euphoria club drug and immediately have a line of volunteers around the block chiming, *I'll have what she's having, please.*

The woman thrashed her head from side to side while complaining, "No. No. No, I just want you to keep making me feel good. Please. Please, Elijah, won't you just keep kissing me and stuff?"

"Yes, of course I will. For as long as you'll let me," I vowed with lips pressed to her throat. But what I really wanted to tell her was that I would love on her forever if she would let me. That I would worship her body and mind and every damn thing there was about her until the end of time.

My eyes fell closed on a ragged inhale. How had I let myself get to this place again? Because I'd sworn I never would. Tirelessly—I'd worked tirelessly to be the kind of guy women could count on for a good time . . . and that was it. I'd made no secret that I was only interested in one thing from an encounter, and when the night was over, we'd go our separate ways. Everyone knew it. Everyone in this whole damn city knew it. Exactly how I'd wanted it to be.

Then came this one. This one woman who lay before me, twisting and turning the best she could in my bindings, begging me to love on her and never stop.

Oh, sweet Hannah, if you only knew how I fought the

demons inside that wanted to eat you alive every time you're beneath me, girl, it would scare you so bad you'd run back to Mommy and Daddy's house as fast as your sexy legs could carry you.

After lavishing her stiff nipples with much-appreciated attention, I decided to pose my next question. The gorgeous siren was panting from a particularly hard bite I'd just scored the underside of her breast with when I asked her, "Are you ready for the next question, beautiful? My God, these tits. I can't get enough of you tonight. I can't figure out what you're doing to me, woman, but it's some kind of potent spell, that's for sure."

"I think it's the other way around, mister. I'm going to die of pleasure overload," she whimpered. "Forget the damn questions and fuck me. Please, I'm begging."

"Oh, that is tempting. Especially when you beg like that. My God. Lift your head and look at how hard you make me." I waited, and she stared at me like she'd had five strong drinks and couldn't coordinate her thoughts and movements.

"Did you hear what I said? Look how hard my cock is for you right now." I waited for her to pick up her head and look across her body to where I knelt over her. I gave myself one long stroke before finishing my thought. "You do this to me."

"Elijah," she whispered. "If you undo these, I can help . . . you . . ." Her breathy entreaty dropped off because I was already shaking my head from the moment I realized where she was going with the plea.

"No way, gorgeous. Are your arms getting stiff?"

"No. But I want to feel you."

"Oh, you will, baby. I promise you will. You're going to feel me in your rib cage when I get inside you."

She moaned and thrashed her head back and forth. "This isn't fair. It hurts inside, I want it so badly. I don't like this anymore. I've never felt like this before, and I'm not sure if it's good or awful." She stared at me, pleading with those big blue eyes the very best she could, and finally whimpered, "Or both?"

"I know, love. I know. You should see how swollen your pussy is." I sat back on my heels and gazed at her luscious cunt. God, it looked so inviting—so plump and wet.

"Please. Please, just do it. I can't take this ache anymore. It hurts in my belly and—"

"That's enough now," I issued quietly.

"But I—"

"I said enough." The second time, my voice was unmistakably serious. And she stopped complaining instantly.

"That's my good girl." I leaned over her and chastely kissed her forehead, not making any other point of contact while doing so, and she whimpered again.

Meeting her wild eyes, I tilted my head to the side in rebuke.

Please, she mouthed without making a sound.

"Do you want the gag, Hannah? Is that what this is about? I'd be happy to use it on you, beautiful. You don't have to manipulate me into doing it. You have to know by now that I'd give you anything you want. Anything that I am capable of giving you, I will. Always."

"No, no, I don't want to be gagged. I just need..." She rolled her eyes back before squeezing them shut. "I need to come so badly it hurts. It actually hurts. You're a goddammed demon, Elijah Banks, and you've barely touched me."

This poor girl was going to pass out if she didn't settle down. Deep-pink splotches decorated her cheeks, and the same sexy, deep-rose color flushed across her chest. The tits I was so enthralled with rose and fell at a pace double her normal, so I covered her mouth with my own and stole her breath, forcing her to breathe a bit slower through her nose.

A rich moan resonated from low in her throat and vibrated through the kiss and into me, doing strange and wonderful things to my whole body. My dick kicked up harder between our bodies, and this time the needy sound came from my own throat.

As I started backing down her body, she opened her mouth to speak, but I stifled her plan with a quick look. She kept her head and neck lifted with her strong swimmer's core and watched me tease my way down her body.

"Nice, baby. Now you get what you need because you've been a good girl. See how that works?"

Hannah finally relaxed and flopped back on the bed, offering a happy, relieved groan to the ceiling. Faintly, I heard her whisper, "Thank you. Thank you. Thank you." Over and over, she kept repeating the gratitude like she had been given a presidential pardon.

"My God, look at you" came tumbling from my own appreciative lips. This woman—this miracle—was so breathtaking in her arousal, not even the finest Renaissance painter would've been able to capture her beauty. The high flush on her skin, the splayed position the bindings held her in, and best of all, the swollen, plump tissue of her sex needing so badly to be satisfied.

I couldn't wait another second. No, I *wouldn't* wait another second.

"Now, my gorgeous woman, is when I want to hear all your words, yes?" A kiss to the inside of one slightly bent knee before I directed, "I want to hear what you want more of"—a kiss to the other knee—"less of what you don't like." Then I rubbed my unshaven cheek down the inside of her thigh toward the heaven I was dying to get inside of. Hannah moaned from the scratchy sensation, so I switched to the other side and gave that leg the same stubbled massage. "Tell me what you like and, of course, what you love. Do you understand?"

She was already nodding eagerly when I had just delivered part of the question, knowing well by that point what I always asked her.

Her voice was raspy and sexy as fuck when she replied, "Yes. Yes, I understand. Please, God, please don't stop. Do whatever you want to me. I love everything you do. Always."

"Oh, baby girl, don't say things you can't take back." My voice was heavy with obscurity, and a shiver danced across my skin, reminding me of that unsatisfied part of me I'd tamped down since Hannah came into my life. Into my bed. She definitely wasn't ready to deal with the dark parts of my kinky preferences. I wasn't sure she'd ever be.

Before she could question the meaning behind my comment—because this girl always asked why, how, or when—I got busy between her legs. Her orgasm was my only focus, and I went at the task like my life depended on it.

Judging by the sounds she was making, I thought maybe Hannah's actually did. Her clit was so swollen, I couldn't resist biting into the tender bud. The sensation between my teeth drove me mad in some animalistic urge to score her with my teeth—to literally mark her there forever so she would always remember who she belonged to.

I knew Hannah wasn't the sort of woman who would respond well to that sort of comment, so even though I was drilling a hole in the mattress with how hard my cock was at the thought of doing it, and telling her about it just beforehand, I had to keep my dark urges to myself. Instead, I sucked harder, licked more, and thrust two fingers deep into her, just trying to quell the need that was consuming me.

My beautiful woman moaned through a long, shuddering climax that left her limp and smiling from ear to ear.

I planted my hands on the mattress on either side of her thighs and bent low so we were nose to nose and growled, "Now, beautiful. I'm going to release you, then lie where you are, and you're going to ride me until you come again. Do you understand me?"

"I-I do. But wait," she said hesitantly as I got to work releasing her bonds.

"What is it?" I couldn't help grinning at the look on her face. You would think I'd asked her to recite the Gettysburg Address from the panicked expression she wore.

"You want me to literally ride . . . on . . . well, I mean, be on top? It's just, normally you're more in control because of . . ." She looked down at my cock, and I knew where she was going with her fumbling thoughts, but her awkward stammering was too adorable to rescue her.

Instead, I threw her further off by asking, "How are your shoulders here? Stiff?" I rubbed the ball portion of the joint where stress might be pulling. If she were going to feel discomfort, that would be the first place. I just wasn't expecting she would, or at least none that she'd admit, so I had to watch her even closer.

"No, not at all. I feel so good right now. That was the best orgasm—oh my God, seriously, I needed that so bad. But you didn't really answer me about this riding you business. I mean, is that going to work with that"—she looked pointedly at my dick again—"monster cock of yours? There. I said it. Happy?"

While she was pushing her own verbal boundaries, I had lain down beside her, slightly propped against the headboard.

"Oh my God, you're too much sometimes." I laughed fully and pulled her on top of me. While she straddled me, I kissed her so deeply, I didn't just take her breath away—I stole it. With my tongue, I stabbed in and out of her mouth rhythmically. Exactly the way I intended on fucking her tight cunt soon.

It didn't take long for her to forget her embarrassment of the conversation she was trying to have and just give in to the feelings of the moment instead.

And if she kept grinding on me the way she was, and gasping and sighing into my mouth, we would be giving in way sooner than I planned.

Cautiously, she wriggled into position. I fingered her entrance, and she was soaked and pliant. If she relaxed and went slow, she could totally take me inside her. It was no different than if I were guiding the action.

"Now, sit up and hold on to the headboard. Oh, fuck yes." I held my dick straight up for my woman's use when she was ready. I muttered the curse as she slowly took my solid cock inside her lush body. Inch by glorious inch.

"See? Just like a couple of days ago in the living room. Look at you, beauty. Look up. Look how hot you are with my cock buried in you. Now you're totally in control of how fast or slow and how deep this goes. Take me, baby. Use me for your pleasure. Whatever I have. It's yours. All that I have, yours. All that I am, yours. All that I feel, yours."

In desperation, she flung her arms from the headboard to around my neck.

"Hold on, sweet thing," I said. "I'm going to fuck you into next week."

"Oh, oh my God, Elijah."

Even though she was technically speaking to me, her head was thrown back as if she were professing her divine enchantment to the ceiling fan.

"Feel good, beauty?"

"So good. I love the way you fill me. It's so much. God, this is better than I could've imagined," she said between rough exhalations.

"Describe to me what you mean," I instructed while roughly fondling her breasts. "Christ, these tits are perfect. Fucking perfect, do you know that?"

She gave a shaky smile and lowered down a bit more, and we both moaned in pleasure.

"Oh, oh shit," Hannah whimpered and closed her eyes, freezing in place for a moment. "You're so deep inside me." She looked down to where I was watching her every move. "Can you feel it?"

Through gritted teeth, I answered, "Yeah, I feel it. But I don't want to come yet, so I'm trying to think of everything but how amazing it feels right now."

"What if I do this?" my bratty woman asked with a glitter of mischief in her eyes. She clenched the inner walls of her pussy, and I thought I saw angels.

Before she could do it again, I gave her a new command. "Lay your body down on mine." I scraped my short nails up and down her spine a few times, and she shivered. I surprised her by rolling us both over as one joined unit so I was on top once again. My cock never left the haven of her pussy through the transition—exactly as I intended.

I ramped her up and then backed off just as she was about to come at least three times, and by the last round, she was nearly in tears. Whether it was emotional frustration or physical discomfort or a combination of the two, I couldn't be sure. What I was certain of, however, was the way her distress turned me on—and in no small way.

I remembered when Grant and I ribbed Bas mercilessly for the way he got hard over making Abbigail cry all the time, and here I was, doing the exact same thing.

"Hannah? Baby, look at me." She was about to come, and the bastard in me had to taunt her just a bit more. "My God, you are so sexy right now. Are you ready to come, sweet girl?"

"Yes! God, please! Please don't stop. Please don't make me wait again. I can't do it again. Please."

Sweat matted long blond strands to her forehead, and she aggressively shook her head from left to right as she told me about her limits. I leaned closer to silence her with a passionate kiss and finished the move by sinking teeth into her bottom lip until she whimpered.

"I believe you can do anything I ask you to do. Don't you?"

"No. No more teasing. Please. Please, I need to come so badly," my beauty panted in her sexy alto voice. The final straw for my resolve was her barely audible, "Just. Fuck. Me." Each word said in time with my hips' thrust as I slammed into her and stole her breath with my big, hard dick.

Every sound in the room fell eerily quiet. After the past hour of fucking and the most erotic flesh symphony I'd ever been a part of, the silence just before her climax was as soundless as the coital celebration itself. Hannah came in an ear-piercingly quiet, all-consuming tsunami kind of climax that rolled through every inch of her body from head to toe.

"Let me hold you," I finally said, or asked, or offered. Hell, I would've begged in that moment, because watching ecstasy dismantle her always did strange things to me. My heart galloped wildly in my chest and then all at once felt like it had stuttered and seized up altogether. I wanted to rub at the pain inside my chest cavity, but Hannah had draped herself atop my body, clueless as to the physical calamity taking place just below.

She had laid her head over the exact spot that hurt, as if she were a human bag balm. Soft waves of her blond hair cascaded around both our shoulders like a queen's robe.

And how fitting was that?

This woman. My queen.

I had to figure out a way to make her stay—stay with me forever. For the first time in my adult life's memory, I lacked the desire to reestablish who was the boss around here. I knew damn well the woman beneath me held my attention a hapless captive when her seductive blue gaze ensnared my sheepy green one. The incessantly tight, heavy balls she led me around by? Yep. Handed those over willingly too.

I was gone for this girl. So fucking gone it didn't make sense anymore, and the only thing I could do was stare at her and grin and hope like hell she either caught the same illness I had or wouldn't mind me staring at her and acting dopey all the time, wondering how the hell I had gotten so lucky. Maybe if I promised to pay all the bills on time and gave her a prescribed number of bone-melting orgasms each month, the plan would work out?

I didn't want to manipulate her into staying with me, but maybe I needed to devise a plan she couldn't resist. When I wasn't careful about the exact phrasing or particular timing of my thoughts, I saw how my unfettered intensity put her on edge. I told myself it was her inexperience and possibly her early childhood trauma.

Treating Hannah like the delicate treasure she was had become very important to me. However, diluting the dominant sway of my bedroom prowess wasn't something I wanted to be forced to do. If that was the only way I could keep her, that would take a different type of inward examination I wasn't sure I was prepared to endure.

I didn't set off on this journey with Grant Twombley one June afternoon in hopes of finding the love of my life. No, I thought I was helping him take care of his lady love and a few of her employees. The last thing I expected was to be navel gazing about my sex-life choices. But if living a long, enriched, love-filled life with Hannah Farsey came at the low, low price of trading one technicolored food pass for a boring, sedate, vanilla one? I'd do it in a fucking microwave mealtime minute.

Every now and then, when I'd been bossy or demanding, a certain look crossed her face that she would quickly hide if she thought I was watching her too closely. It couldn't be helped, though, and she would have to start dealing with the facts. For one thing, she was gorgeous. Simply stunning. I constantly wondered what this beautiful goddess saw in a man like me, because as I saw it, she was so out of my league. Pointing it out constantly was just dumb, though. I didn't need to plant negative juju in our backyard garden.

Secondly, by its very nature, being a dominant male meant I took care of my woman. In all things. Seeing to her physical well-being was as important as ensuring her emotional needs were met and her mental health goals were tracking in the right direction, too. Simply stated, I wanted to own her. Body, mind, and soul.

Physically being near Hannah brought those traits right to the surface. These things were happening long before I intentionally or unintentionally was part of a conversation like this one.

Once I was willing to turn inward and see my own behavior and hear my own language for what it was, I recognized the signposts pretty fast. Because I had experience in a long-term relationship before, the moment I started feeling the negative emotions on deck like jealousy, frustration, and suspicion, I vowed to address them at the first available opportunity. Left unaddressed, those somewhat small insecurities could poison and eventually destroy the entire relationship.

I needed to care for her and provide for her. The feelings I felt for Hannah were like being in a time warp to my past. I hadn't felt this way for another person since Hensley Pritchett walked out on me. Truth be told, I didn't think I'd ever feel this way again. I hadn't been looking for a woman to fill the girlfriend shoes in my life. Hell, I'd kicked that pair to the way back of my closet where they were lost under years of other things I didn't want to bother with. But my sexy girl had dug them out, dusted them off, and slid her feet right in.

And what do you know? The pair fit my beauty perfectly.

CHAPTER FOUR

HANNAH

Drops of water plopped from his tight muscular frame to form two puddles on the pool deck. His face was buried in a white towel as he dried the excess running off his hair and down into his icy green eyes. Eyes that would search for me in the next moment or two because I wasn't where he'd seen me last.

As ridiculous as it sounded, it really had gotten that intense. Because my beautiful man's possessiveness had ballooned into its current overinflated state over a period of time, it hadn't seemed as suffocating to me as it probably should have.

Usually, the scale noticeably ratcheted up only when a dangerous situation arose. After one of those episodes, trying to reason his ownership vibe away was pointless—with Elijah or anyone else, for that matter. Considering his primary peer examples were Sebastian Shark and Grant Twombley, any other behavior would've been unanticipated.

The first had his wife carted off to a Mohave Desert safe house when he was overly paranoid his secret enemies would turn their sights on her. The second one nearly strangled his woman while she slept beside him, mistaking her for the same secret enemies who were trying to hurt Shark by hurting the people he cared about most. Grant had terrible PTSD-driven nightmares from the week and a half he spent in their captivity. So now, everyone in that man's circle of close friends was just trying to stay out of harm's way and undo the mental and emotional damage that had already been done.

Including me. I was trying not to add stress in any way, shape, or form to Elijah's life. If he ended up spending another decade man-whoring around the greater Los Angeles area, it would not be with my name on his lips. No matter what it took, I would not be the one he blamed. If things didn't work out between us the way he envisioned, it wasn't going to be my reputation he dragged through the mud and then in and out of every willing woman's bedroom.

When I was a girl, my father always preached to us about the importance of a good reputation. That your name could make or break you before you even entered a room. So even though LA was a huge city, when you were born and raised here, and then as an adult lived and made a living here too, that same gigantic city was somehow reduced in size.

It was rare to go out and not see someone I knew. Either a family friend, someone I went to culinary school with, or even someone who was one of my sisters' friends. My father worked very hard to make a good name for himself and our family over the years. We all understood what that meant and did our share to keep it that way as we got older and stepped out into society.

Although I feared for Shep's ability to color inside the lines for much longer, I had to trust that most of her issues were with me personally and not my parents or other sisters. For whatever reason, if she wanted to hurt someone, I felt confident it would be me she took aim at and not my mom and dad.

Sheppard would be the one person not happy to see me later today. But first, I needed to deal with the dripping, sexy dilemma right in front of me. I couldn't predict Elijah's reaction to the news bomb I was about to drop on him, but I'd seen him function under pressure before.

Not only was he arrestingly handsome to observe while having a normal conversation, but also experiencing this man in a passionate exchange with another person was like watching the different stages of an active volcano bubble and burp until it finally erupted and molten lava boiled out over the rim.

He wore my favorite cocky-but-oh-so-sexy grin as he strode over to the kitchen slider, still dripping from his swim. I slid the door back to see if I could get him anything from inside while he dried off. However, his answer evaporated into the morning sunbeams along with the moisture in my mouth.

At least a dozen things ran through my mind regarding the tight and fabulous clenching sensation in my abdomen and parts lower while I stared at the way his practice suit hung so low on his hips that it was just shy of obscene.

"Jesus Christ, man," I muttered and closed my eyes, playing it off that the sun was causing a terrible glare as it bounced off the other windows around the courtyard.

"You're so full of shit." He chuckled. "I saw you checking me out." His eyes glimmered with the same mischief that tugged his grin wider.

I raised my chin in defiance. "So what if I was? You have some nerve, mister, strutting around here like that." I made a sloppy gesture with my hand, starting down low at his toes and sweeping up the length of his body.

"Did you have a good swim?" I inquired.

"I did. Thank you for asking. You know you're always welcome to join me, don't you?"

"Yes, and I appreciate that. I think you'd pass me in no time though, and I'd feel like I was in the way. You know what that's like, right? When someone's up your ass in the same lane you're practicing?"

"Yes, the worst. But my God"—he rolled his eyes dramatically—"what I would give to be up your ass, Ms. Farsey. You have no idea." Elijah groaned and took a deep breath, fluttering his ridiculously long eyelashes as he let his lids fall closed. When he popped them open again, he took an exaggerated inhale through his nose like he was recentering his chakras and picked up the conversation where he had stopped before.

My God, help me. I think I could fall in love with this man.

"Makes for a stressful workout, though, you're right. But hey, talk about motivation, right? Before you know it, your time in the pool is done!"

"I don't know . . ." I started a thought but trailed off as I considered my options. "I'd rather work out alone and do it at my own pace than with a group and be pushed past my limits."

"That's my practical girl," he said and tried to pull me close into his embrace, but I batted at his outstretched arms.

"No way, man. You're still wet, and I don't want to change again before I head out." Here we go. It was now or never. He just loaded the bases, and I was going to hit the grand slam to bring all the runners home. Or send me home, as it would be in this case. I chuckled at the absurdity of the word game taking place in my mind but sobered quickly. There wasn't a single funny thing about what I was preparing to do.

My handsome man caught on to the little verbal clue I

had just dropped and was giving me that curious puppy stare with the tilted head and all. If his hair were just a bit drier, it would be flopping to the side in that irresistible way it did.

Inquisition and confrontation morphed his features and bearing before my eyes. "Hannah? What's going on?" he finally asked.

I let out a big sigh and ran my toe along one of the grout lines of the tiled floor. How was I going to say these words if I couldn't even maintain eye contact with him? But there was no point putting it off any longer.

"We should probably talk." With a sigh, I looked up and asked hopefully, "Do you want to sit down?"

"Not really, no. Just say what's on your mind." Tension pulled his spine even straighter, and he seemed to grow taller by an inch or two.

"I'm going to go home today. Back to my parents' house." There. Mic drop. That wasn't so bad.

"The hell you are."

"Elijah, I'm serious."

"Great. So am I."

"Please don't fight me on this. There hasn't been a security issue for weeks now. Not even a stray photographer." It sounded so logical coming out of my mouth, but when I had to stand and look at his crestfallen expression, there was no way to stop the pain in my chest.

"This doesn't mean we're not going to still see each other," I added quickly, hoping I could address all the negative points he might try to make before any one of them had a chance to gain wings.

"Really, beautiful? How do you see it playing out? Me coming over to your mom and dad's place and we all hug it out on the sofa all night long?"

I chuckled at the thought, because again, the visual those words painted was downright silly. But it was the perfect segue to a point I wanted to address.

"Of course that's not what I had in mind, but while we're on the subject, let's talk about my folks."

"Maybe I should sit down after all," Elijah grumbled, but I heard him just fine.

"They're two of the nicest people you'll ever meet. But that's the problem here. Or one of the problems."

He looked at me like I switched languages midsentence and finally found one he didn't have working knowledge of.

"I'm not following your logic, beautiful."

"The problem is you haven't met them. Ever. Typically, when one of us wants to date, that happens first, not after we've lived with the guy for a few months. This whole thing"—I made a wide lasso around my head to encompass our unusual situation—"is really out of the ordinary. I think it is for most people."

"I'd like to take a moment to point out that I wanted to meet your parents when you went back to their house to pack some things. It was, I don't know . . ." He looked upward like the answer he was searching for would be written on the ceiling's hand-troweled plaster. "Maybe the second or third night after you moved in. Do you remember that?"

I nodded but got the very distinct impression he'd plow on whether I had or not.

"And you said no. You said it would raise too many questions, and you were adamant about it. And I respected you on the matter." Now that he'd gotten all that bluster out of his system, he crossed his defined arms across his chest and leaned back. So fucking cocky, like he had scored the final blow.

It was true. I had said those things, and it really would have caused quite a stir if I had shown up with Mr. Gorgeous here and said, *Oh, it's okay, Daddy. He sneaks into my room at night and does amazing things with his fingers.* Yep! I was sure he'd be totally understanding if I just told the truth like that.

With a hint of new intention in his gaze, he stepped toward me. No, he sauntered or maybe prowled—those were the best ways to describe the seductive way his body moved closer to me. Scooping my hands into his own, he brought my fingers to his plush lips and kissed them.

"So what do you propose we do to fix this situation?" His green eyes looked like they were painted with watercolors today. Probably a result of the delightful amount of sun that lit up the west-facing side of the house.

"Why do you have to move back in their home permanently for me to meet them? Let's invite the family here for dinner or something. You can show off your new home," Elijah said, trying to sell the idea. I had a feeling he wasn't going to go down without a fight on this.

"Can we agree on a few conditions that might necessitate my return instead?"

His eyebrows seemed to be climbing with their own agenda as intrigue distorted his face.

I wanted to laugh or at least chuckle, but I could see what all of this was doing to him, and it definitely wasn't funny. But seeing Elijah Banks with a confused expression was like a Bigfoot sighting. Rare. After thinking about it for just a moment, I realized why he was resisting something that really wasn't the big deal he was making it into.

"How much of this"—I made a sweeping gesture up and

down his body—"has to do with the fact that you feel out of control right now? None of this was your idea, and it makes you uncomfortable, nervous, or some other negative feeling."

"None," he answered quickly. Maybe a little too quickly. I'd have to circle back to this point because I was pretty sure there was a giant tangle beneath the surface if I just pulled on the loose thread that was visible. But we were on a timeline for the rest of the day if we were going to make it to dinner on time.

"You going to let me in on this conversation or just have it with yourself?" He chuckled at his quip, and I gave him a cheerleader smile, as he called them. Fake and forced with no true emotional fuel behind the expression. "I'm going to get out of this wet bathing suit. Come with me to the bedroom so we can continue talking?"

The last was poised with the lilt of a question, so I followed him down the long hall from the kitchen to his master bedroom. As we walked, I tried to explain the meaning of my first comment.

"I'm hoping if I go back and it's completely unbearable with my sisters—fine, with Sheppard—or just living by my parents' rules now that I've had a taste of life out from under their wings..." I shrugged sheepishly, feeling very self-conscious all of a sudden. "I don't know..." I couldn't meet his gaze, so I studied the turquoise nail polish ID let Rio paint on my toes for Abbi's wedding. Finally, I said, "Maybe this is too much to ask." I seriously wanted to tuck into a ball and roll out of the room.

"Please just say what you were going to say before you sabotaged yourself."

"Okay. Okay." I held my hand up to stop him from anymore of the Elijah Banks tough-love style of encouragement. It wasn't always easy to explain to someone who counseled as fiercely as they loved and labored that some situations were better suited for a gentler hand.

So instead, I fortified myself with a deep inhale and just blurted, "Can I come back?" I scanned his features for immediate signs of rejection. Not noticing any, I explained further. "If it doesn't work out at my parents', I mean. I'll understand if you say no, because I realize how presumptuous it is of me to think there's a perpetual welcome mat at your front door with my name on it."

I could hear my rambling. I could feel my cheeks' temperature climbing much faster than the rest of my face. I could even picture myself shifting nervously from one foot to the other and then tried to stop that too when I imagined how silly I looked.

Times like this, it was hard to imagine why anyone bothered having me in their life. I was a serious train wreck who monopolized conversations, people's attention and time.

From outside my body, I witnessed it all but still couldn't stop the disaster. I lived with the potential implosion every day. Today just happened to be *the* day the train went off the tracks.

Waaaaayy off the tracks.

With my face shielded by my own hands from more humiliation, I started in with the apologies. I could hear my heart pounding in my ears and feel it like a heavy bass line at my clavicle. From behind the safety wall of my hands, the remorse and recrimination were easier to start heaping on. If I had to look at his perfect face while admitting all my imperfections, I would have never gotten through even one round of apologizing.

Left, right. Left, right, repeat. Left, right, left, right, again. I shook my head in desperate frustration. "I'm sorry. I shouldn't have asked. I feel like an idiot." I put my hand up in a *stop* gesture so he wouldn't consider letting me off the hook. "Forget I said anything, okay? Can we just forget that happened?"

Before I could say anything more, Elijah took me in his strong arms and held me tightly against his body. The moment I felt his sedate bearing wash over me too, I sagged against him. Heaven. He felt and smelled like heaven, and it was effortless to sink into him completely.

God, I was going to miss this. Miss him *when he left me.*

"Hannah, listen to me. I don't want you to leave at all." He dipped down so we were at even height and looking at one another, eye to eye. "Do you understand what I'm saying to you? Don't leave. Whatever it is you need or whatever I'm not doing, I'm sure it's something we can work out. But baby, I can't fix what I didn't know was broken." His eyes had thawed from the typical ice to a mossy green like nature's carpet that sprouted up between the rocks outside his back gate.

"Tell me what you need," he beseeched. "Tell me how to make it better."

"That's just it, and I'm trying to explain it to you, but I know I'm doing a terrible job. I'm not your responsibility." I stopped talking abruptly, even though there were plenty of things I still wanted to say.

A strange sound came from low in the man's throat or possibly from his chest somewhere. He sounded like an animal on the hunt or one that was cornered and getting very testy about it.

"Are you growling? Like legit growling at me right now?" I took a step back, and he immediately advanced into that space. I took another step back and felt the solid support of the king-size mattress behind my legs. Again, Elijah filled the emptiness, trapping me between the bed and his body.

"How can you say something so ridiculous?" He leaned over me, and I tried to angle back. One more degree of tilt, though, and I would be flat on my back on his bed.

And why did I feel like the cornered animal now?

"Wh-What? What did I say?"

"You're not my *responsibility*?" He nearly spit the word like it was sharp and bitter on his tongue. "Maybe—maybe not like a job or paying taxes. But in here"—he got his hand in the small void between our bodies and thumped on his chest—"in here, I feel like I need to protect you. I need to take care of you. Provide for you. When I do those things? Those basic things? Then I feel like I'm living my perfect life. Those are the most basic elements of me. I don't know if any of that makes sense. And I'm aware of how much of a caveman that makes me sound. Maybe even simpleminded. But that is my truth."

Straightening, he paced away, and I stood up tall again as well. Watched with my jaw hanging open a tad in reaction to everything he just declared. Stretched my neck as far as possible when he disappeared around the corner and into his closet to pull on some jeans and a well-worn T-shirt.

"Sit with me a minute? I'm not sure when you wanted to leave, and I really hope you will reconsider leaving, period. But I won't force to you to stay if it's not what you want. Even though every cell in my body is clamoring to do exactly that."

In the sitting area of his bedroom, we both took a spot on the love seat and angled our bodies toward each other. Elijah scooped my hands into his and lovingly stroked my skin.

"I want to share something about my past with you that very few people know. It may help you understand why I have such a deep-rooted need to care for you."

"O-o-kay. Thank you. I won't betray you," I offered in response and tried to hold his gaze, but for the first time since I'd met this breathtaking man, he wouldn't make eye contact with me. So unusual. "Elijah?"

But still he stared at our joined hands, and I could almost hear how many thoughts were trying to break free from his complicated mind.

"When I was a child, my mother and father seemed so in love, you know? At least, it seemed that way to the outside world, and really, to me too. Especially when I was a young boy. My father treated my mother like a queen. When he came home from business trips, he always had lavish gifts for her. Sometimes for me too if she gave him"—he made air quotes—"a good report when they spoke on the phone."

I smiled at the thought of a young boy with Elijah's arresting good looks. Those electric green eyes and charming smile—I'd have to ask him to see some photos another time. Instead, I asked, "What did he do for a living? Your father . . ." I was trying to remember if I'd ever heard his name used.

"He was an art broker. Paintings, sculptures, and illustrations mostly. At the time, graphic art was in its infancy, and the performing arts, well, obviously, that's a whole different business."

"How fascinating. And exciting. And you never wanted to follow in your father's footsteps?"

"No."

"Ummm, okay." I had a feeling there was a much bigger story to that one-word answer, and it was very clear I wasn't going to be hearing it. At least not right now.

"The reason I brought up that son of a bitch wasn't to

take a sweet stroll down memory lane with you. Shit, I don't know why I led off this conversation with words about that gutter rat." Elijah sprang to his feet so aggressively, I yelped in surprise.

"Sorry," he muttered with barely a check over his shoulder to ensure I was okay.

Wow. Something about his father really triggered his temper. I was compelled to stand and go to him. Comfort him. But honestly, I felt nervous from the way he was acting.

Only a couple of minutes passed, and then my handsome man sat down beside me again. He had schooled his rage or shame, or whatever emotion that was, and wordlessly asked for my hands again. I gave him my entire body instead by climbing into his lap and wrapping my arms around his neck. Ensuring we kept our stares locked, I linked my fingers together behind his head and pressed my forehead to his.

"I'm so sorry you had to remember things you didn't want to. I feel like I was the catalyst, and I'm so sorry."

"Hannah, my beautiful, beautiful Hannah. Don't be ridiculous." A sly grin started in the corner of his plush mouth and seductively spread across the distance.

I'd seen this trick before and knew he was about to tease me in one way or another.

"Obviously, you're an amazing woman."

My grin was as wide as his then, just waiting for the punch line.

"But even you can't influence people's minds. Sorry to burst your bubble, babe."

I playfully narrowed my gaze at his. "Really?"

"Really."

With both sets of fingertips up to my temples, I performed

a charade of a person in deep concentration. "Do you feel me?" I giggled while asking.

"I feel something, but I don't think it's what you were going for," he growled in a deep tone and banded an arm across my back to hold me very close while he pushed his semi-erect cock up into me.

"You are insatiable," I said through my chuckles.

Elijah stopped all motion and was very serious. He waited until he had my complete attention. No more shitty thoughts about his father, no more silly thoughts of sexy times that would make us late. He set me back on the love seat cushion in my original spot.

He turned and faced me fully while saying, "I owe you an apology." Any further with the trajectory he was on, and he would've been on his knees between mine.

With his perfect face in my palms, I asked, "What are you talking about? Apology for what?"

"I truly wanted to share something with you. I should've left him out of the conversation. I know better because every memory involving that bastard turns sour in my mouth. His ghost has no business in the same room where your light is. Never again if I can help it."

"Okay..." The word dripped with skepticism but went perfectly with the side-eye I shot his way. He sounded a touch unhinged, but I didn't think now was the best time to point that out.

Instead, I made overexaggerated gestures while I spoke, falling back on my camp counselor training from three hundred thirty-four years ago.

"Let's brush this family drama under the rug right here and move away from it." I pointed down to my bare feet, using larger than necessary hand and head gestures. But it worked like a charm because he was following every broom sweep and thumb hitch I made. I finished with a mime sequence made of dusting off my hands, surveying my pretend handiwork, and giving myself a generous nod of approval. I grabbed the collar of his T-shirt and tugged him in for a kiss to wrap the whole scene up.

Silly me.

Elijah crashed into my mouth with a passionate kiss and didn't release me for several minutes. Eventually, when he did step away, like a yo-yo on a string, he snapped right back to me and pressed his perfect lips to mine once more. No kissing this time, though. Instead, he gave a profound promise that I would never forget. No matter what happened between us down the road, I would never forget this moment.

Full, commanding, demanding lips melded into mine. "I'm never going to let you go." Elijah bent down to even our lines of sight. "Do you understand what I'm saying to you?"

Taking a couple of vital seconds to breathe, I nodded and stared. Stared and fell deeper. Harder? I wasn't sure what the painful part of this equation would eventually feel like, but the very little bit of experience I had with men warned me it was going to be terrible when it did. No, scratch that. Devastating sounded more appropriate.

My God, help me. I'm falling in love with this man.

Did there have to be a bad part? Did I dare bring up the ten-car pileup equivalent of couple's conversation topics with him? Maybe if we survived this family meet-and-greet tonight and no one lost an eye or any other vital body part, I could muster up the courage to talk about our future.

My stomach twisted in several knots at the thought of a

Where do you see us in five years? talk with this man. But like every other time I was upset or anxious, he disarmed me with his captivatingly good looks and incapacitated me with his commanding demeanor. I never wanted him to change a thing.

When he was in this mood—demanding yet sexy and playful—I could feel a current of raw emotion humming at a low frequency right beneath the surface of his normal vivacity. It was as if he were waiting to feel something bigger or more intensely, but he didn't know what, so he was unsettled. Almost jumpy. If action didn't come to him, he went on the prowl—searching for the stimulation, the right combination of words or circumstance. It was exhilarating almost to the point of frightening to be caught up in the vortex of this man.

And I finally figured it out. Why the danger of not knowing what was around the next bend in the road was such a big thrill when I was with Elijah, when all my life I avoided those types of situations like the plague. Because Elijah always got behind the wheel. He was always in control, and I liked it that way.

I didn't have to worry about taking care of him because he took care of himself *and* me. He *wanted* to take care of me. I wasn't a burden or a nuisance to him like I felt with nearly everyone else in my life. And no amount of therapy could wash it away. The guilt was hardwired in my mental conduit.

"You were going to explain this inherent need to care for a woman."

"Not a woman. You. Hannah." He kissed my left eyelid right after it fluttered closed.

The involuntary response was my body's way of showing gratitude for the delicious rasp in his voice. Between the warmth of his mouth on my skin and the sound of him saying my name with just the right measure of command and just the right degree of entreaty, I could feel a dark, needy pulse all the way down in my pussy.

"Rochelle." My perfect lover dragged slow, burning kisses up and over the bridge of my nose to the other eyelid.

"Farsey." Lastly, he pressed seeking lips to mine, and instantly, I parted for him. He didn't waste time with more warm-up either. Just dived in and thrust his tongue halfway down my throat on the crest of my moan. Before I could comprehend what was happening, both his arms were around me, and he moved my body under his strong, potent one.

The love seat wasn't long enough to accommodate our bodies by half, so when he released my mouth for an urgent breath, I realized he had moved us to the floor. As much as I wanted to go a round of dirty fucking before I finished getting ready, I knew a round could last hours with this man.

But he was on a mission and went straight for my kill zone, kissing and licking my ear, neck, and then moving downward. With his hips, he made ridiculous, thought-scrambling circles against my pussy. The barrier made of my jeans and the pair he'd just pulled on was the only thing in the way of a completely carnal connection.

I really couldn't give up any amount of time. I'd scheduled the dinner at my parents' house to celebrate my homecoming, technically making me the host. When I sneaked a glance at my watch and quickly calculated the commute from Malibu to Brentwood, I was completely into the emergency reserve minutes on my timetable.

My mom always insisted on being put to work, so when I'd called to set up the plans earlier that morning, I'd given her a grocery list to shop for before we arrived. She'd let me know that my sisters Maye and Clemson had invited their boyfriends, so we were going to have a nice, full house. The phone line had vibrated with her happiness and excitement at having such a full table for a nonholiday meal.

But that gave me an idea. It was playing a little dirty, but sometimes a girl had to do what a girl had to do.

"Oh my God." I gave the comment some extra whine. "We should've been in the shower like . . . ten minutes ago. Do you think you can start peeling the carrots in the produce drawer while I'm in the shower?"

I tried to maneuver out of his embrace, but he had me in a vise grip.

"I'd walk over hot coals for you," he offered in a voice so raspy I had to maneuver my clit around on the inside seam of my jeans to get at least some sort of stimulation.

He knew just by watching the expressions change on my face there was a war going on between my brain and my libido, and the battleground's hotbed was right between my thighs. I was so damn horny, and if he didn't move his ass and get in the shower . . .

Elijah, of course, had no intention of behaving.

Holding my gaze, he moved off me but issued a simple, "Stay."

Without warning, he crammed his hand into the front of my jeans and immediately growled.

I squeezed my eyes shut tightly, as though it would put a stop to the delicious madness.

"Jesus Christ, Hannah. You're so fucking wet. Let me take care of this, love." He tugged at the moorings of my button fly, getting three of the five open before I regained enough sanity to stop him.

"I can't believe I'm going to say this, but no." I cuffed his wrist with my hand and said, "Not now. Rain check?"

He picked his head up from the crook of my neck to meet my stare. The green of his irises was frosty and bright with lust and need.

"I absolutely need to taste you, Hannah. Right fucking now."

"No. We don't have time."

"No, beauty. This is happening. Where's your phone?"

Confused, I answered, "There on the bed, I think?"

"Stay," he issued again, coupled with a serious look, and quickly got up, dashed across the room, grabbed my phone, and was back beside me on the floor of the bedroom's sitting space.

"Unlock." He held my phone in front of me for the facial recognition feature to unlock the screen and quickly typed a message while I watched.

Every time I started asking a question, he silenced me with a serious and stern look. I heard the sent message chime sound, and he tossed my phone onto the sofa.

"Now be a good girl and enjoy it like you're supposed to. I just bought us twenty minutes, but the sooner you're satisfied, the sooner we can leave. If I smell like your cunt when I meet your parents, well . . ." He shrugged like he had zero cares about the idea. "Now about this wet pussy." He deftly found my clit and circled it with firm pressure.

"Elijah—"

"Unless you're screaming my name or saying *yes, more*, or *that's so good* . . ."

He locked my attention on to him. His voice, his smell, the beautiful cocky grin plastered across his lips. He knew he had me. He knew there was no way I'd turn him away now. Because we both knew how much he disliked lying, so as usual, he was totally telling the truth. My panties were wetter than I could ever remember them being.

It only took a few minutes for my orgasm to hit me like a fierce storm. My entire body trembled from the release, and my muscles felt like JELL-O afterward.

Elijah rested his head on my thigh, and I stroked my fingers through his hair until I contacted his scalp with my nails. He loved when I ran my fingernails across his head—said it was relaxing. So when his grin stretched so wide it was visible regardless of the fact he was facedown in my lap, unconsciously, mine stretched that wide too.

My God, help me. I am in love with this man.

I wanted to tell him. Just blurt it out and let the chips fall where they may. Of course, I didn't.

Nor would I.

Elijah was still the same man who had the Los Angeles notoriety of fuck 'em and leave 'em. I'd be a fool to think this sheltered daddy's girl could change the man whore or his philandering ways. For whatever reason, he was on a charity pilgrimage with me, and it was that simple. More than likely, as a favor to his best friend, Grant. That made the most sense, since that was how he came into my life in the first place.

I wanted to curl up against Elijah's warm body and take a nap like we so often did after fooling around in the daytime, but I knew I was already on borrowed time. I wanted to ask him who he'd texted and what he'd said, but I was trying to make a valiant effort at trusting him, so I held my tongue.

A quick lip-lock to wrap up our alone time before we hopped into the shower and got ready. I had to dodge his advances and grabby hands while making sure I rinsed the conditioner from the depths of my long, thick hair. At our current pace, we'd be calling my parents with some lame excuse and instructing them to call Grubhub instead of having a home-cooked meal.

My gorgeous boyfriend emerged from his closet in body-hugging—but not tight—dark denim jeans. He wore the most handsome pair of caramel-colored wingtips that I had ever seen. The tips of the toes and the heels were a darkening gradient of the same tone. It made me think of a Siamese cat with its points.

The cat personality pretty much fit the man standing before me, too. My God ... if I could read minds ... I wondered if I'd want to know what he was thinking in that moment while I stared at him with open appreciation then nervously fidgeted with my own outfit.

I went with an olive-green flight suit that was a high-end designer replica of the one-piece coveralls fighter pilots wore. When I first got the suit, I wasn't really sure about the look on me, but every time I wore it, I got so many compliments, so I figured why not?

I wanted to feel confident tonight, and I wanted to have my game face locked in place in case Sheppard started in on me. She usually loved embarrassing me in front of friends I brought home to introduce to our parents. Unfortunately, I usually played right into her hand.

I planned on having a talk about her habit with Elijah on our drive to my parents' house so he knew what to expect. I certainly didn't fear for his integrity, though. My guy could hold his own against the worthiest opponent.

Out in the garage, Elijah saw all the stuff I had packed in the back seat of my car earlier that afternoon. Again, with that ridiculous growling sound. There were occasions when it was hot and sexy, but this wasn't one of those.

"Stop it." I scowled and hit his chest with the backs of four fingers. Good Christ, the man was a solid wall. I narrowed my eyes and tried to look serious. "For real."

But my posture was already wilting right alongside my mood, because I knew by his body language I'd just hit a hornet's nest with a Wiffle ball bat. So, I braced for the impending showdown. I'd be damned if he was going to woo me with sex this time. I was on to his pattern now, and when all else failed, he came at me with that magic wand of his, and I was dusted. Not this time, though. I was ready. Mental chastity belt locked and loaded.

Instead, he calmly said, "Do you want me to drive separately?"

What the hell?

That was the fastest flip-flop this man had ever executed for my benefit. So while my stare seemed exceptionally appropriate to me, to Elijah it must have extended into the boundaries of *concerning*.

He gripped me by the tops of my arms, his hands so much larger than my frame that he could encompass the entire ball of my shoulder with his palm. The hold was much more than necessary to garner my attention, so he was either much more agitated than he was letting on, or the man was just that clueless about his own strength.

My bet was on the former.

"You're hurting me," I spat through clenched teeth.

There was some sort of memory clawing at my chest. Pushing down so I couldn't breathe. It would sit there and become heavier and heavier. I knew it. I fucking knew it. By the time I realized what was coming, it was too late to save myself.

I can't breathe. "You're hurting me," I cry, but his ugly smile just gets uglier. *My throat is closing in on itself.* "I can't breathe," I whisper so I won't use as much air. *My vision is getting smaller, and that doesn't make sense. I have excellent eyesight. Daddy always says I do. Daddy says I am his perfect little girl. Not anymore. Not when he finds out about this.*

Why? Why is he doing this? Kick. Kick. Scream. But I can't. His palm is over my mouth, and it smells bad. No. No. Stop this. I don't want this. I need air.

"You're hurting me!" I shout when he shifts to unbuckle his belt. Finally, he lets go of my shoulder, and I yell loud enough to make him stop.

"Kick. Kick, kick as hard as you can! If anyone ever tries to hurt you again like those people in the bathroom on your birthday, you kick and scream and do everything you can to attract attention. Kick like you do in the pool," my daddy encouraged when we talked about this awful stuff. I got really quiet, which he took for my serious face. He didn't know it was my petrified face and that I'd already peed in my pants when he came into my room and said we needed to have a grown-up talk.

I was sure they'd found out. He and Mommy found out, and they were going to give me away just like the man said they would if I ever told. I was going to have to figure out what to do with my jeans and bedding when he left.

"Fuck! Hannah! Come on, baby. Breathe, please. Look at me. I don't know what to do. I don't know how to help you. Please, beautiful girl. Please look at me."

Elijah's strong, clear voice broke through the traumatic flashback, and it came crashing to an end. Thank God. But then the realization hit me. I couldn't level my gaze with his.

I started rocking in place. I wasn't even sure where that was . . .

Oh no.

No. Not again.

I was so afraid to look up and see exactly where I was. It was always the worst part of these. Discovering who witnessed it happen this time. Now there was another person in on my secret. Another person I'd have to explain things I didn't understand myself. Another person . . . who would know what a sham I was.

CHAPTER FIVE

ELIJAH

"Then at least let me drive," I insisted, and honestly, if she didn't relent, I had every intention of throwing her over my shoulder and carrying her back inside. Dinner with her family be damned. "There is no way you should be behind the wheel right now. For one thing, look how badly you're shaking."

We both looked down to her trembling hands, and she quickly stuffed them into the hip pockets of her flight suit.

Stuffing my hands in atop hers, I tugged her body against mine. "I love this outfit, by the way. You should wear these one-piece jumpsuits more often. Your body was made for them."

I made an obvious show of looking around to the back of her and checking out her ass, desperate to get her mind off what just happened here. I knew it was inappropriate to be talking about her tight, delicious body at a time like this, but I also knew she needed something else to focus on in the moment, because clearly we were not canceling this godforsaken dinner with her folks. If she wanted to go, she was going to have to pull her shit together so we could make our best showing.

"Are you going to mime for the rest of the evening?"

"Stop being an asshole. There. How's that?" She nipped the words in my direction.

"Unnecessary, for one thing." I stared at her in challenge.

I understood her nerves were a bit frazzled, but I didn't have an *Everlast* label sewn on my forehead.

"In the spirit of not losing more minutes, because I know you want to arrive on time, I can have Lorenzo or Marc bring your car to your parents' later tonight or tomorrow. But right now, he's driving us so I can give you my undivided attention."

"I didn't ask for more attention, did I?"

"What you're going to end up with is a bright-red ass." I leaned closer and kissed her forehead. "Lose the attitude, my beautiful queen. Do you have everything from inside? I'm going to lock up."

"Where is the box that was on the island? That was dessert."

"Already in the car."

"And the wine? There were like four bottles, I think?"

"Car."

"All right, that should be everything." She wiped her palms on her thighs and took a deep breath. I couldn't remember seeing her this nervous about anything. Not even launching a freaking hot-air balloon.

I hustled through locking up the house and was beside her in the back of the SUV in no time. We had about thirty minutes on the road in good traffic conditions, and the weekends were downright unpredictable, so we had to just see what we got into as it happened.

Since that episode in the garage before we'd left, I'd been thinking about the gentlest way to bring it up again. I was confident she wouldn't do it on her own, so I had to approach it in a way that felt safe for her.

In my limited experience when I actually cared about how I interacted with a woman emotionally, it seemed like putting my own neck on the chopping block. As if I said, *See, honey? I can bare my soul emotionally to you. Won't you do the same?*

The part that sucked with my theory was the obvious— baring my own soul first. But for one thing, I had plenty of shitty parts of my soul I could bare. Also, Hannah was worth it. She would always be worth it.

There was something so generous and pure about her that made me want to tell her my entire life story. Minute by godforsaken minute, right up to the moment I walked into Abstract Catering and saw that thick blond braid down the middle of her back. I would maybe skim over all the thoughts I had in *that* exact moment but then jump back into the rest. I wanted to tell her all of it.

The impulse was unfamiliar and took me by surprise. Even when I gave myself to Hensley completely—body, mind, soul—there were still bits and pieces I held back. I always assumed I would tell her those remaining details eventually. Getting the big chunks out was hard enough. What did the little embellishments here and there really matter? But something never felt quite right. Deep down, I always felt like I was hiding things from her. Like those last bits of information would send her packing, and it never felt right. Because I knew lies by omission were still lies.

I had picked up on a habit of Hannah's, though, and I had to be careful not to fall into her trap, because I thought I already had. Maybe twice. She was an expert at conversationally steering attention away from herself and getting someone else to talk about what they had going on. People were usually so lonely or hungry to talk about themselves, they didn't notice that she had rerouted the conversation one hundred eighty degrees. Avoidance of her by rapt attention on you—clever and effective at the same time.

As we drove out of the neighborhood, Hannah stared out the window like it was the first time she'd been on the block and didn't want to miss a single thing.

I had her hand in mine and gave it a squeeze, hoping she'd look at me.

It wasn't immediate, but finally, she did.

"Thank you for inviting me. I'm looking forward to finally meeting the Farsey posse."

Her answering smile was paper thin, and I didn't think it was stress about cooking that was getting to her.

"Are we sticking with the house-sitting story?" I asked. "Since that's what you got off the ground with?"

"Probably would be easier, don't you think? Less chance of crossing details."

"Okay. But on principle, you know that I . . ."

Hannah put her hand up in a full stop gesture. "I know. I know. You don't appreciate lying, liars, any form of not being honest. Christ, I get it."

I just stared at the woman.

"What?" she finally snapped.

"Are you going to hold on to this mood all night?"

"What if I am?"

"I know you were going to try to avoid getting into an altercation with one of your sisters in general, but the energy coming off you is so confrontational, Hannah, everyone will think we were fighting the entire way over."

"So you're actually worried what everyone thinks about you?"

"One more, beautiful. That's all that's left," I said conversationally while gazing out the window on my side of the vehicle. She heard me loud and clear, though.

"One more? What does that mean?"

I looked at her and then tilted my head to the side until my hair lost the battle with gravity and flopped over too. She knew she was pushing my limits, and she knew what I was talking about when I warned her that I had patience left for only one more rude comment before she was over my knee. The head tilt and hair flop was just to antagonize her because she said it drove her crazy.

"You don't scare me, Mr. Banks," she challenged.

"Good. I'm not trying to. And I appreciate the deference. Thank you." I winked for good measure.

Through gritted teeth, Hannah said, "You can be so infuriating."

"So I've been told." I waited for a moment or two but then realized this might be the only segue into the topic I really wanted to discuss with her.

"I think I've always had that effect on people. When I was a boy, I used to make my father so mad, and it would be over the dumbest things. It took a long time as an adult, and shit"—I chuckled, and none of what I was saying was even close to funny—"a lot of hours on my therapist's couch, to understand none of it was my fault."

About halfway through my confession, she turned her face toward me. Her heart was too kind to not give compassion when listening to a story like this one.

"Would you get put on restriction?"

"No. I was much younger when it started—at least as I've been able to remember. I worked with a psychologist for a long time to dig up memories my brain buried."

"Why?"

I looked at her with a puzzled expression. "What do you mean *why*?"

"Why dig all of that up? If your brain was trying to hide it from you, there must have been a reason. Why go against what nature intended?"

"Because my brain started letting out bits and pieces of the memories when I would least expect it, and of course never when it was convenient to have a breakdown after feeling like I had a nightmare while I was wide awake." With a deep exhale, I finally looked at her, not sure what I'd see.

Hannah reached for my hand to comfort me.

"I know this all probably sounds crazy. Maybe I should stop talking." This was the exact place I'd hoped she would start confessing that she was going through the same thing.

Instead, she covered my hand with her other one and held them in a tight stack.

"It doesn't sound crazy. Not at all. I've heard about dream regression therapy, and it sounds fascinating. It doesn't work for everyone, but I'm glad it did for you. Did it allow you to make peace with the past and move on? The article I read said that was a major benefit. Patients dealing with PTSD got a second chance to deal with trauma they hadn't dealt with when it happened—for whatever reason—and heal and move forward."

After thinking about my answer for a moment, I went with the real one. No use sugarcoating it.

"I have to be honest with you. It wasn't a quick fix. I was young, for one thing, so it was hard for me to relax enough to let the process work. Once I saw the results, I was actually anxious to go to therapy every week." I laughed again, and she smiled in response.

It instantly warmed my heart to see her genuinely smile again, and I realized how completely enthralled I was with this woman. Not that I didn't know it before, but to put my emotions side by side with hers on a timeline with such a short interval really highlighted the intensity of my feelings.

Hannah gave my hand a squeeze and asked, "Hey, are you okay? We don't have to talk about this anymore if it's making you uncomfortable."

"No, sorry. My mind was wandering. When I started remembering things, things I thought were nightmares from the past, I realized they were actually flashbacks." I shrugged. "Or memories, I guess, from when I was a boy." The lump in my throat made it difficult to breathe, never mind speak, and I needed a moment before I could talk again. It was a biological wonder the way our brains protected us from events too devastating for our little hearts to remember.

I lifted our still-joined hands to my lips and kissed the back of hers. I just wanted the reassurance that she was here in front of me—that this wasn't something I was remembering.

"Let's talk about something else. It hurts my heart to see you upset like this," she insisted in a gentle and calm voice. If someone heard just the tone of her normally sultry, alto voice, they would think she was talking to a napping infant.

"No, beautiful, I'm not upset. The days of that man upsetting me are long gone. It's just that remembering those things is still difficult. It was my own father, you know? The man I looked up to. The man I had built an altar of worship to in my little-boy brain." I swallowed with difficulty and felt a hot, fat tear roll down my cheek.

"And the whole time, he was really just a monster."

Two more tears followed in the path of their trailblazing

brother. I didn't bother wiping them away. I wasn't too proud to cry in front of Hannah. If she hadn't realized before how serious I was about being vulnerable with each other, she would now. She could trust me enough to open up completely. Like I just had with her.

Lead by example and all that happy horseshit.

Before I could process what she was doing... and stop her, Hannah had disengaged her seat belt and launched herself into my arms. Her style of comforting someone was full frontal. Meaning you got all of her in your arms, on your lap, around your neck, any way she could manage. Just another thing I adored about this girl. The list was getting so long I was going to need paper by the roll to keep track of it all.

"What are you doing?" I pulled my head out of the crook of her neck, which happened to be one of my favorite places to rest my face these days, so I could see her studying me.

"I think you're trying to break my heart. I will do anything and everything in my power to never see you cry again." She put her hand up in a stop gesture before I even said a word. "And not because I think men aren't supposed to cry. I just don't like seeing you upset to the degree that elicits tears."

"I'm definitely not trying to upset you," I said. "I thought it might be helpful to share something from my past. Maybe a similar experience to what you just went through"—I thumbed over my shoulder as if pointing back to the house in Malibu—"in the garage. Then maybe you would want to share with me too. You would know you're not the only one going through something like that. It's not uncommon. There are even people, professionals, who can help."

Moments passed. Moments that felt like hours. Hannah just stared at me. Still sitting on my lap but disengaging from my embrace, and eventually moving off my lap and back into her own seat, and locking her seat belt in place.

"What?" I asked her, maintaining direct eye contact while doing so.

"Did you really just say that to me?"

"Say what, exactly? Spell it out for me so I don't misunderstand you."

"Don't be obtuse."

I mouthed the word *obtuse* with my eyebrows hiked to my hairline. I couldn't help the grin that spread across my lips afterward, either.

A few silent seconds hung in the air between us before I finally spoke again. "Seriously, Hannah, what did I say that offended you? I think you're so used to everyone tiptoeing around you and not forcing you to deal with the hard stuff, so the hard stuff never gets resolved. How close am I to the truth?"

"I don't know. You tell me. You seem to have all the answers." She folded her arms across her chest and exhaled with a lot of frustration. "You think you have it all figured out, don't you?"

"No. Just the opposite. Because you keep me in the dark, I have no answers. I'm trying to put pieces together that don't fit." I motioned in front of myself like a merchant showing his wares. "And this is the dangerous result of that game. Wires get crossed, words get misunderstood, feelings get trampled on."

"Well, nothing is going to be resolved now. This is my street."

"Your parents' street," I muttered under my breath.

"Whatever. Put your game face on, *boyfriend*." She all but snarled the title. "You have a family to impress."

The moment we were both out of the SUV, I wrapped

my large hand around her throat and pushed her against the vehicle.

Wisely, Lorenzo said nothing and went around the other side to give us some privacy.

I lunged my knee between her thighs, nearly lifting her off the ground and very effectively pinning her in place. With my lips right beside her ear, I growled so only she could hear me.

"You are in for the fucking of your life when we get home tonight. You'll be lucky if you can walk tomorrow. I was going to leave it up to you, but I just made the decision for you. You're coming home with me tonight. Where you belong."

I waited for the defiance I knew she would level at me.

"Are you grinding your pussy on my leg? You filthy girl. Never can get enough, is that it? Good news for you. Open." I thrust two fingers into her mouth, and she immediately closed around them and sucked.

"I've had it with this mouth too, mmm, yes. You like that, don't you? Now I have all evening to think of what I'm going to do to this hole too. No. Don't stop now. Maybe next time you'll think about being so disrespectful, even after I repeatedly asked you to check yourself." I ground my erection into her belly, and she moaned around my fingers.

"Open." I pulled my fingers out and wiped them carelessly on her jumpsuit, just over her breast. "Now, put your game face on and show Mommy and Daddy what a good girl you really are. And tonight, when we get home, to *our* home, I'll show you—the only fucking person who matters in this world to me—what an amazing, giving boyfriend I really can be."

Her pulse thrummed in her neck. I could feel the chaotic pounding beneath my grasp. The wild, glazed look in her eyes was an aphrodisiac of its own. But now wasn't the time to be thinking of that. I needed to settle my shit down before I could meet her parents for the first time. It wouldn't make such a great first impression to have a giant boner the first time I shook her dad's hand.

"Holy shit, man. You are lethal."

She was talking to me but busying herself with grabbing her bag and the dessert from the vehicle.

"Baby, let me get that, please."

"Can you grab the bottles of wine?" She looked back over her shoulder as she started up the walk from the driveway.

Lorenzo intercepted the dessert directly from her hands while she was turned back and looking at me.

"Nice play, man," I called to our driver.

"No worries. The wine is already by the front door. Just text me when you're ready to go home."

"Thank you, Lorenzo. You're the best." Hannah bumped the man's shoulder with her own, and he actually looked bashful.

Christ—this woman was having a strange effect on all the men of my household.

And not one was complaining.

The front door swung open as we came up the walk, and the cacophony you'd expect from a football stadium–sized crowd washed out from inside.

"Hannah!" A middle-aged woman bustled out, wiping her hands on her apron, and collided with my girlfriend with a world-class hug.

I shot my arms out to steady them because it looked like they might actually topple to the ground from the enthusiastic embrace.

Goddamn, what I wouldn't give for someone to be that

happy to see me. Even once in my life.

I didn't realize how long I must have been staring or how dopey of a look I must have had on my face until a tall man said from beside me, "I've seen them take each other to the ground more than once."

Slowly, I turned left, and a handsome man-version of Hannah greeted me. A tall man, somewhere between my height and Grant's, stood with his hand outstretched in greeting.

"Dave Farsey. How's it going?"

"Hey. Elijah Banks. Pleasure meeting you. Hannah's told me so much about you."

"Is that right? Why hasn't she said a single word about you?" The man inspected me with knowing eyes as we shook.

He wasn't being unkind necessarily, but he was definitely pissing on the trees in his yard. I, on the other hand, didn't feel the need to mark my territory. I'd already claimed what was mine, and she'd be leaving with me when this night was over.

With perfect timing, Hannah appeared at my side.

Her voice was filled with respect when she asked, "Daddy, you've met Elijah?"

He bent to kiss his oldest daughter's cheek. "I have, dear. How are you, baby? You look positively radiant tonight. Just glowing."

"Isn't she? I was saying the same thing," the woman said, still clutching Hannah as though she couldn't bear to let go.

"Will you two stop? Elijah, this is my mom, Lisa." My girl's blue eyes sparkled in the porch light as she looked from one parent to the other.

"It's a pleasure to meet you," I said and took her mother's outstretched hand. "Thank you for having us tonight."

"Nonsense. This is Hannah's home. Any friend of hers is

always welcome. Let's go inside," her mother cooed, and like little ducklings, we all followed her into the house.

Already, the place was filled with the smells of a busy kitchen while a much-too-loud television played in the adjoining great room.

"David," Hannah's mother said in the tone of voice wives used to chastise their husbands in front of company. "Can you please turn that down? I can hardly hear myself think."

With an eye roll for my benefit, he said, "I doubt you're missing much." But the man went to hunt for the remote, moving at least five throw pillows before finding the thing between the sofa cushions.

Three other blond girls milled around the kitchen, and Hannah introduced me to her sisters. First up were the twins, Sheppard and Maye. Maye's boyfriend was by her side, and he shook my hand but didn't have much to say other than a quick hello.

The third sister was lingering at the end of the island with her guy, and I guessed correctly that it was Clemson. Her boyfriend looked like a swim team member, and I asked the pair a few questions about how the season was shaping up.

"Banks!" Her dad bellowed so loud, I jumped at the issuance of my name. "What are you drinking, son?"

I shot a look to Hannah because we hadn't discussed this protocol. I had to assume if she didn't want me knocking a couple back with her dad, she would've made a bigger point of letting me know so we wouldn't be in this exact situation.

Sticking with a universally safe answer, I said, "Whatever you're having, sir," and walked toward the wet bar, where he poured clear liquid into a glass with about eight ice cubes. It didn't give me much of a visual clue until he topped it off with tonic and a lime wedge. I was safe in guessing gin and tonic. Not my favorite, but not too bad, either. At least it wasn't some syrupy girly drink like a tequila sunrise or a daiquiri.

"See what you think," he said and thrust a glass toward me.

I was hoping the edge of impatience I thought I was hearing was my oversensitive peacekeeper tendencies at work. I reminded myself to check that shit at the door. I didn't know these people at all, and saddling them with my baggage wasn't fair.

This perfectly lovely family had no idea that I had a compulsion to keep the peace so desperately that I would just about stand on my head and shuffle a deck of cards with my toes if it meant defusing an argument bomb. Especially one that started with some imagined shortcoming of my mother's and ended at the explosive powder keg of my father's temper.

As I got older, the lengths I would go to in order to keep her safe got more and more extreme. His violence was spinning out of control, and like any junkie, his tolerance was growing by the day. What had once been the limit of what he could justify doing to her had become just his warm-up.

All that talk about my childhood with Hannah as we drove here had my brain running in five different directions. Wasn't a feeling I was overly fond of, especially around this many unfamiliar people. Rather than make a comment I would regret or have held against me later, I took a slow drink from my glass and let the fizzy liquid bubble in the back of my throat.

"What do you do for a living?" I asked the man of the house, hoping to change the topic to safer and more stable ground.

"Oh, nothing too exciting. I'm a CPA, just like my dad,

and his dad, and his dad. I specialize in wealth management, though, and that's a modern-day subset in the profession. Such a thing didn't exist back when they were counting beans."

"Can I ask, are your parents still with you?"

"No, unfortunately they aren't. My father died of a cardiac arrest after a routine procedure, and my mother lived about ten years without him and just passed away about a year ago."

"I'm really sorry to hear that. I'm glad Hannah had so much time with her grandparents, though. I think family is such a vital part of our lives."

"Do you have a large family?"

"No. Just me at this point. Both parents are gone, and my grandparents are estranged, so the people I consider family are not blood related."

"Nothing wrong with that. As long as they come when you call, right?"

"That's how I see it too." And so the conversation went until I excused myself to use the bathroom and just have a few moments to myself. I wanted to stab myself in the eye with the first sharp—or, hell, it didn't matter if it was blunt—object I could find to do enough damage to have an excuse to leave.

But when I came back into the great room and saw my stunning woman chatting and laughing with her sisters and mom, I just stopped and watched her. She was so damn beautiful and happy. The kitchen was her kingdom, and she ruled the land like the queen she was, setting all her loyal subjects to tasks to help bring the meal to the table on time. She really was glowing tonight, and my heart gave a painful lurch in my chest. Was she this happy because she was here with her family?

Maybe this really was where she belonged and not on a

beachside cliff in Malibu. I thought I was giving her everything she needed, but I wasn't sure she'd ever looked this happy at my place.

Our place, as I had come to think of it.

It was no secret that I didn't always do the right thing when it came to moral fortitude. I sure as hell didn't have the answer here. If leaving her here tonight when this meal was over and driving back to the coast alone was the right thing to do, I was too damn selfish to do it.

One of the twins—not the cranky one, so it must have been Maye—noticed me standing in the shadows and alerted my beauty. She looked up from the pot she was stirring and gave me the sultriest look. I wanted to knock every dish and glass off the long table and feast on her perfect body right there instead.

"Mama, can you stir this? It's done. I just don't want it to stick before the pasta is done." She made the wooden spoon handoff and was on her way across the room to me.

Captivated. There was no other word to describe how I felt in that moment. Spellbound maybe. Smitten for sure worked, but mesmerized fit better. Captivated seemed to circle the lot and come down right in the middle of all the physical and emotional sensations coursing through my body all at the same time. Had I ever felt this way for another human before? Woman or man?

No.

It was that simple. No. I probably never would. There was no way you were gifted a second person who fit you so perfectly ... so completely ... in one lifetime. One was already more than you could hope for. One who, when you found her, *if* you found her, you dug in with all ten fingers and all ten toes. Hell, I'd happily bite into her with all my teeth if it were socially acceptable—just to make sure she never got away.

"Gorgeous man," she said coyly when she got within arm's reach.

As usual, her mere nearness scrambled my brain, and I completely forgot where we were. I snaked my arm around her waist and pulled her against my body with such a forceful tug, we both made an *umph* sound when we collided. Distantly I noticed the nonstop chatter in the kitchen completely shut down, but it wasn't alarming enough to make me take my eyes off this queen.

"How's it going? Is my dad giving you the third degree over cocktails?" She smiled up at me and made no protesting attempt to escape my embrace.

"Nothing I can't handle. I have to say, it's been a while since I've met a girl's parents, though. I hope I'm making a good impression."

"I've seen how charming you can be. I'm sure there's nothing to worry about. Are you hungry?"

I gave her a quick head-to-toe sweep and asked, "For you? Always. What did you have in mind?"

She smacked my abdomen with the back of her hand while saying, "I'm talking about dinner. God." She chuckled and shook her head. "You're insatiable."

I held her hand in mine so there could be no more physical abuse and pulled her in closer. "Only for you," I said and kissed her softly. "And yes, whatever you're making smells amazing. Can I do anything to help?"

"No, everything is under control. We're going to get this masterpiece on the table in a few minutes, though, so let me get back in the kitchen and work my magic."

Pulling her against me, I leaned down and said beside her

ear, "Woman, I've been spellbound since the moment I met you." I kissed her neck just below her ear and then stood tall again, assessing her reaction to my words. My heart and ego swelled when I saw the starry-eyed look she was giving me.

"My God, you have the silver tongue tonight, Mr. Banks." She started backing away but didn't let go of my hand so our arms were stretched between us.

"Just tonight?" I asked with her favorite head tilt.

"Oh my God. I can't with you anymore." She dropped my hand and spun around to go back to the kitchen, where every female Farsey present stood staring with the same goofy lovestruck look on their face. I was ecstatic to see the excitement they shared with their sister and the way they giggled and teased her when she came back into the kitchen.

Dave was beside me when I snapped my attention back to my own surroundings instead of Hannah's.

"I'm not sure I've ever seen her so smitten," he said, looking across the room at the women. Fatherly pride radiated from the man like the warmth of the summer sun. "What are your intentions, exactly?"

Shit. I was so thankful I hadn't taken a slug from my drink because I might have choked when hearing that one. Intentions? Did we just time travel back to 1950?

"Intentions, sir?"

"I realize the phrase is a bit outdated, but I can tell you're a smart man. What are your plans with my daughter? For the future?"

"Well, ultimately that will be up to her. Right now, we're dating and letting things run their natural course."

"Are you sleeping together?" the man asked, tone never changing from the conversational one he had been using our entire chat.

"Sir?" I, on the other hand, sounded like a teen going through puberty when my voice cracked on the monosyllabic word.

Farsey raised his graying brows and answered my question with a question. "Which part of that didn't you understand?"

"Probably why you're asking it in the first place," I forced through a laugh, but he didn't join in. *Jesus, is it getting hot in here?* "Hannah's twenty-six years old. I'd say she makes her own decisions on what she does, when and who she does it with, no?"

"Well, here's the thing. I'm guessing you know about her past, and things have been a little unusual because of that trauma. Her mother and I have always been very protective." While his words were direct, they weren't threatening or unkind. He was a father looking out for the best interests of his child.

Albeit a capable, independent, incredibly smart, and brave adult child. But child all the same.

"Maybe a little overprotective?" I couldn't hold the comment back. I didn't want the man to think I was a pushover. He should know I would stand up for his daughter if the situation called for it.

"Maybe, at times. We don't want to see her hurt. She's had enough of that to last a lifetime," he replied quietly.

"I can assure you that is the last thing I want to see happen to your daughter as well. I will do everything in my power to ensure it doesn't."

"Who's ready to eat?" Mrs. Farsey called from the kitchen as she escorted a parade of the next generation to the table, all carrying steaming dishes.

The other two boyfriends who had been huddled near the

television since arriving came to the table and took the chairs beside their mates, Maye and the youngest sister, Clemson.

I'd been wondering how they'd escaped the fatherly grilling that I was being subjected to, but after the older of the two had sneaked me a couple of sympathetic nods, I figured the dude had already put in his time in the hot seat.

I waited by Hannah's chair to help her get settled before I took the place beside her. "This smells divine. Nice work." I gave her knee a quick squeeze under the table, and she grinned wider.

"That's one I haven't seen before," I said for only her ears.

Hannah looked at me quizzically.

"That particular smile. Trying to figure out what it means."

"I'm just . . ." She lifted her shoulders and then let them drop, grinning the whole time. "Happy. Happy to be here with my family. With you. All together."

The words were in my mouth. They were right there. I was on the verge of fumbling the moment in front of her entire family, but thank God someone else at the table stole the spotlight.

Christ, what was I thinking? I needed to get a grip on myself. All these family vibes were leaking into my psyche or something.

"Hey. You okay?" Hannah asked so only I could hear.

Just as quietly, I answered, "Yep. Perfect. Why?"

"You look pale all of a sudden. You sure?"

"I think the drink just hit my empty stomach. Just need some food." I leaned in and kissed her just below the ear and kept the affection appropriate for the dinner table.

Food was passed around, and conversation flowed from one subject to another. I learned a little about each of my girlfriend's sisters—except for Sheppard, who basically pouted her way through the meal and moved her food around on her plate and never really ate much of it. Apparently I wasn't the only one who noticed.

"What's wrong, Shep? Not hungry?" Dave asked his daughter.

"Don't start with me, please," she answered with a scowl.

"I'm not starting anything. I simply asked a question." Mr. Farsey kept his tone even and nonconfrontational, but the air in the room thickened with tension.

Lisa shot her husband a pleading look, to which he gave her some sort of nonverbal reply. It always amazed me how couples who had been together for many years could have entire conversations without actually speaking.

This one was her saying *Just leave her alone. Don't start this in front of company.*

His look back said *I'm tired of this bullshit. This is my house, and she needs to show some respect.*

Okay, so I filled in what I would've said in that situation, but Dave Farsey was a take-no-bullshit kind of guy from what I could tell. I knew Hannah said they all treated him with kid gloves because he had sensitive blood pressure and a resulting cardiac condition, but the guy seemed fit as a fiddle to me and probably resented all these women treating him like he was weak or broken.

Maye attempted to smooth things over for her twin, something I had a feeling she did often. I'd have to check the theory out with Hannah later.

"Sheppard, if you don't eat your dinner, you won't have the dessert Hannibal brought with her. It looks ammaaaazing." The more gregarious twin singsonged her opinion of the dessert we arrived with.

"You can have mine, Maye Day. I can't do any more time at the gym this week," Sheppard said, pulling her smartphone from beneath the table.

But the young woman was so reed thin, it was hard to imagine she had any extra energy to get to the kitchen to clear her uneaten meal into the trash, let alone go to the gym to work out.

At least two voices came in chorus, "No phones at the table!"

Hannah's mother spoke up. "Sheppard, you can have dessert if you want."

With deafening volume, Clemson objected immediately. "No, that's not fair!"

In my peripheral vision, I saw Hannah wince and, just past my girlfriend, caught her mother doing the same.

But the youngest would ensure justice prevailed.

"The rule is no dinner, no dessert. Why are you making exceptions to that rule now? Why is everyone always afraid to upset Shepp Errrd?" She pronounced her sister's name in two very hard and distinct-sounding syllables, one more bitter than the first.

"She's a bitch no matter what anyone does, so who cares?" she finalized.

"Clemson Nicole!" Lisa chastised. "Close your mouth this instant!"

The maverick gave a one-shoulder shrug. "You know I'm telling the truth." She pointedly scanned up one side of the table and down the other until she landed on her boyfriend's shell-shocked but utterly smitten face. Dude probably had a boner for his Joan of Arc below the dinner table that very instant. She gave him a quick wink, probably not realizing we were all still glued to her every unpredictable move, and Hannah let out a snicker.

Aaaannnnddd apparently that was all it took.

"I'm out of here!" Sheppard aggressively balled her napkin, slam-dunked it onto her full plate, and bolted from the dinner table.

"I'll go talk to her." Hannah immediately volunteered to fall on the sword, and I was about to object—straight-out refuse to allow her to be that sister's whipping post in order to keep the peace—when Maye stood up.

"No, Han, let me. I know how things get between the two of you. No offense." The pretty girl retracted her head into her shoulders like a turtle into its shell after making the comment. "I think I stand the best chance of not needing stitches when all is said and done." She gave her boyfriend a regretful look, and he squeezed her hand in support.

What a freaking schmuck, letting her go into that battle zone unarmed. At least freaking go with her. I don't know. Family dynamics were hard to understand and very touchy to get involved in. They had the twin thing—the bond or whatever—to contend with on top of everything else. Maybe the chump knew what he was doing by lagging behind.

"Come on, Joel. You can help me with the recycling." Dave summoned the abandoned boyfriend to help with a chore, and I couldn't have been happier to not be roped into more alone time with the patriarch.

"I'll help you clean up here," I told Hannah.

Everyone started talking between themselves, and the door between the garage and house burst open.

"Shit! Am I too late? I'm soooo sorry, guys. Fucking

traffic in this town, I swear!"

"Agatha! Please with the swearing. For heaven's sake, we have company!" Mrs. Farsey looked across the room before cradling her head in her palms. "Where did we go wrong, David? I swear, I gave them all I had."

"You were a wonderful mother, dear. The best." As if that was his cue, the man was across the space to her, whisking her into his arms to comfort her, even if the whole bit was drama in the first degree.

Still, Lisa Farsey looked up to her considerably taller husband as though he would straighten the belt around Orion's midsection tonight—while his girls slept safely under his roof—simply because she mentioned it looked crooked earlier.

Goals. Right there. It was clear where Hannah's notion of what to expect from a relationship had come from. But man, the guy was setting the bar impossibly high. Or maybe those were my own insecurities coming to the head of the line, because when I looked around the room at the other two boyfriends, they didn't seem to have a care in the world. They were under as much pressure as I was because of this show-off and his perfect husbandness, yet I was the only one watching this public display of gallantry and getting more stressed by the second. Seriously?

Hannah ducked under my arm to take a hug from me rather than wait for me to wrap her in one. She really had the cutest habits sometimes.

"Why don't you visit with Agatha and your family, and this other breather and I will clean this up?"

"Oh my God, what did you just call him?"

"A breather. Like that's all he's doing, although even that is becoming questionable. How are these other two guys so relaxed and carefree around your dad? I thought he was going to hook me up to a polygraph over there." I gestured with my chin while carrying dirty dishes into the kitchen behind her.

She set down the plates she was carrying and looked at me with deep concern. "You mean he didn't get to that before the meal? Well, I guess I'll do the dishes myself. You're not done with him after all." And she was totally serious. She gave me a sympathetic pat on the back and went back toward the dinner table.

But I snagged her arm and tugged her back into the kitchen. "Wait."

"Don't be nervous, babe. You abhor lying, right? You'll do great." She actually gave my stomach a reassuring pat like I was a puppy and stretched up to kiss my cheek. "I think he said he's shortened the test recently, so you shouldn't be too long."

Right then, Agatha came into the kitchen, and Hannah rushed to give her a hug.

"Hannah, I'm the worst. I'm sorry I missed dinner. I sat on the fucking 405 for almost two hours. Goddamn construction."

"Don't worry about it. Buuuuut . . ." She drew out the word as she turned toward me and tugged her sister with her. "I want you to meet Elijah. Elijah, this is my oldest sister, Agatha."

"Hi." I shook her hand, but she looked at me with a puzzled expression.

"What's wrong, dude? You look like you just got the worst news ever."

"Oh, Dad and his lie detector test." Hannah shook her head in dismissal and rolled her eyes for extra good measure.

Agatha jumped right in on discounting the man's behavior. "Oh . . . don't mind him." She squeezed my forearm and leaned in like we were sharing a good laugh. "He's harmless."

I shifted my gaze down to where she was still gripping my arm then up to Hannah and quickly to her sister. Jesus Christ, how did this night go from kind of okay to really not good in such a short time?

After what seemed like five minutes of extremely awkward silence and Hannah's sister gripping my arm like her life depended on it, Hannah burst out laughing, and her sister fell in with her. Okay, I was definitely missing something, but I could definitely use a good laugh at the moment.

"Oh my God," my beauty said, wiping tears from her cheeks. "Oh my God."

"Shit, that was funny," Agatha said. "That was the best ever. But I think," she said, pointing toward me, "you are in so much trouble. Someone doesn't look too amused."

CHAPTER SIX

HANNAH

"So when are you going to tell the rest of the family?" I leaned against the headboard of my old bed while Agatha rummaged through her drawer, looking for a pair of pajamas. She'd taken a quick shower and wanted to be comfortable, and I couldn't blame her. But she had also just dropped a big news bomb in my lap, so I decided to pivot my plans on the spot.

I was so thankful I had covered my bases with Elijah before we left the Malibu house and he had already decreed I was coming back home with him tonight no matter what. Things were just falling into place from every angle. I decided to take it as a sign from the universe that I was doing the right thing.

"Well, I wanted to talk about it at dinner, but since I missed that opportunity completely, I'll probably just talk to Mom and Dad tonight after you guys leave," she said, pulling the thermal top over her head.

"I'm really excited for you, Dah. You're going to love being out of this house. I know I do. It would be hard to live here now, I think. Even if I weren't with Elijah, I don't think I could live with the family anymore."

"Have they worked it out yet? That he is the one you are supposedly house-sitting for? That you're really shacking up with that god of a man?"

I couldn't help but giggle. I mean, my man was heavenly, in all the ways, but I knew the toad had his warts too. To hear my sister call him a god just seemed silly.

"No, and I'd appreciate it if that information stayed between us. I don't think they would like it very much. Dad's been giving him the business all night. Elijah's been a good sport about it, but I'm not sure how much more he can take. In fact," I said, standing and stretching, "I better get out there and rescue him. Dad is liable to really hook him up to a polygraph."

"Will you help me find an apartment?" Agatha asked as we went toward the great room. "I started looking on my lunch break, but I've only been able to look at two places, and they were both nos."

I could hear Elijah's deep voice among the others in the room, and my stomach did a little flip-flop. My God, what this man did to me.

"Oh, yeah, sure. Why were they nos, though?" I asked, trying to get a better sense of what she was looking for in an apartment.

My sister wrinkled her nose in distaste. "One was in a really bad neighborhood, so now I know not to look at addresses on that street, and the other one was so small, there's just no way I could handle that."

"Well, you may have to lower your expectations if you're not going to have roommates. I understand rent is very high in that part of town," I offered, playing my role of the older, wiser sister.

Agatha linked her arm in mine. "See? This is why I need your help."

I gave her a squeeze and found Elijah's gaze on us from

across the room. I mouthed to him *Are you ready?*, and he stood immediately. I had to grin at his exuberance at the first mention of leaving. Poor guy. I'd have to be extra sweet to him tonight for being such a good sport.

With an outstretched hand, my boyfriend said good night to my parents. "Mr. and Mrs. Farsey, thank you so much for having us tonight. It was a pleasure meeting you."

"Elijah, of course," my mother said, taking Elijah into her arms for a hug.

He looked a bit surprised but returned her gesture. I watched with affection as he said goodbye to my sisters and their boyfriends, and in no time, we were in the back of the SUV and heading west to Malibu.

"I never realized how loud that house is until tonight." Wiggling my index finger in one ear, I continued explaining, "My ears are actually ringing right now. You know like when you leave a concert?"

"It's definitely a lively household," he said diplomatically. "Do you think I made a good impression on them?"

"Absolutely. I can't wait to get the morning phone call and hear all about it. Although, with the bomb Agatha is probably dropping on them right about now, I'm not sure you will be the number-one topic."

"Why? What's going on? She's great, by the way. I can see why she's the sister you're closest with. Not just because you're closest in age. And Clemson . . ." He threw his head back and laughed, and I had to smile too. "I love that girl."

"Yes, Ms. Clemson has that effect on a lot of people. She definitely has brass balls, doesn't she?" I asked, beaming with pride.

"That's putting it mildly. That boyfriend of hers has

his hands full. But instinct tells me she's running that dude into the ground on a daily basis. And I think he likes it that way." He shook his head, still grinning.

"What's so funny?" I asked.

"Just to be that young again. She's a lucky young lady. You all are." His demeanor changed on a dime, and a very serious mood settled over him as he turned to watch the passing traffic on the far side of the freeway.

Leaning my head on his shoulder, I enjoyed the quiet of the vehicle and warmth of his body beside me. Finally I asked, "You seemed to just get very sad. What are you thinking about?"

"Sorry." He kissed the top of my head. "I don't want to bring your mood down." Eventually, he added, "I'm fine."

"You're not bringing me down. I like when you share what's on your mind." I studied his features while I replied. Or at least what I could see of them in the dark back seat. The bright lights over the freeway flashed in and out of the tinted windows as we sped beneath them, so it was more like seeing him in a dreamscape.

"Really, it's nothing. Sometimes I wonder what my life would've been like."

"What do you mean? Would've been like if what?"

"If things had been different. Different choices, I guess. Different parents." He let out a heavy sigh and stroked my cheek. "Seriously, we don't have to talk about this. It's all so maudlin."

"Please, talk to me. If you want to get something out of your head, or your heart, you can trust me to listen. I want you to believe that."

"I do, beautiful. I do. It's just..." He paused for a long

moment, and I wasn't sure if he was searching for the right words or if he was debating continuing with his thought track. "Nothing good comes of digging up old ghosts."

"Except the only way to banish ghosts is to face them head on."

"Is that what you've done?" he challenged.

At first, I bristled because his words felt very combative. Almost accusatory. Especially as I flashed back to the episode I had in the garage before we left for dinner tonight. But I took a calming breath and reminded myself I'd just vowed to be supportive, and flying off the handle because I felt defensive wasn't the way to show support, was it?

"I've tried to. At least with the demons I know. Granted, there seems to be something I'm not fully aware of that's trying to make itself known to me, but yeah, the bad stuff I do know that happened in my past . . . I've tried to face and make peace with. And no, it hasn't always been easy."

"I think you're so brave. And probably much more so than I am."

"Why would you say that?" I asked him, completely puzzled. "I think you would slay every dragon that threatened me or our kingdom. Without question. At least, that's the way I feel when I'm with you." I shrugged, then ended with, "Safe."

Elijah gave me the warmest smile. "Good. I want you to feel safe with me. And you're right, I would destroy anyone or anything that tried to hurt you. You have my word on that."

"Then let me slay yours."

"I don't have any."

"I don't think you're being honest with me right now." I knew I was treading on very thin ice, basically calling this man a liar after he had repeatedly denounced lying in any and every form.

The sideways look he shot my way confirmed I'd hit a nerve.

So I backpedaled a bit. "What I mean is, I don't think you're being honest with yourself. There seems to be something in here"—I reached across and put my flat palm over his heart. I could feel how strong and virile the man was beneath my hand—"that's bothering you this evening, but I'm not going to push you. If you feel like you want to tell me, you'll tell me."

There. Was I using guilt as a tactic? Maybe. But if it worked, maybe the underhanded method would be worth it. I was navigating in uncharted waters here. All I knew was I didn't like seeing him this troubled, and it was unusual. Elijah was normally rock-solid. It was actually nice to be the solid one for a change instead of the needy one.

"I'm glad traffic's light tonight," he said.

Thankful for the darkness in the car, I freely rolled my eyes. Really? We were talking about traffic now? What next? The weather? The rest of the car ride home was quiet, and maybe that was what we both needed.

When we got off the freeway, Elijah finally spoke up. "You didn't tell me what Agatha's news was."

"Oh, you're right. I guess I got sidetracked. She's moving out of our family home. She wants to get a place closer to work. She said that commute is killing her, and I don't blame her. You know how the 405 can be."

"Yeah, that freeway can be brutal. Well, that's exciting news. But she was the main reason you wanted to move back home, right? Because you were missing spending time with her. Where does that leave you?"

Leave it to my man not to miss that detail. A slow smile crossed my lips. "Well, I wanted to talk to you about that.

I don't think I can tell my parents just yet about our living situation, but are you still open to me staying with you?"

He gave me that damn head tilt and hair flop combo that sucked the air from my lungs every time and said, "Do you even have to ask?"

"Well, I don't want to take anything for granted."

Thankfully we pulled into the garage at that exact moment, because my stomach was doing crazy flip-flops and I needed fresh air. I didn't know why I was so nervous about bringing the topic up with him.

"When do you think you'll be ready to move the rest of your stuff in?" My gorgeous man wrapped me in his arms before we went inside the house.

"Well, I wanted my parents to get used to the idea of us dating first before I break the news to them that I'm living with you. I don't want my dad to have another heart attack, and I think news like that will stress him out too much."

"Can I speak freely here for a second?" he interrupted.

"Of course. Always. I think we should have a standing rule to always have that safe place with each other."

"I think the women of the house aren't giving that man enough credit. For one thing, he's fit as a fiddle. For another thing, if everyone is so worried about his health, maybe he should cut back on the liquid courage." He raised his eyebrows skeptically, and I couldn't deny the logic in what he was saying.

"Oh, believe me, my mom rides him about the drinking, but he does rule that roost in all ways, no matter what it looks like to the visitors." I deepened my voice to mock my father's. "If I want a cocktail at the end of the day, I'm going to have one, damn it." Then I changed back to my own voice to finish my thought. "His words exactly if you can't tell." I playfully bumped my shoulder into his chest. "Please open the door before my bladder bursts."

"Really?" he asked, mischief glittering in his eyes.

"What is that look for? I've seen that look before . . ."

"Oh, we could have a lot of fun right now."

I narrowed my eyes and tried to work through what he could possibly be talking about and came up empty. Clearly this was something my inexperienced mind didn't understand.

"I don't think I want to know what you're talking about, since the only thing I said was with regard to peeing."

Something about that comment made him laugh out loud, but at least the door was open, and I hustled down the hall to the powder room and took care of business before he got any other crazy ideas. At least I knew what the next Google search was going to be on my computer. If I dared.

Just thinking about all the things I had experienced since coming and staying here with him blew my mind. Six months ago, if someone had told me that I'd be staying in a beachfront mansion in Malibu with one of the most eligible bachelors in the country, I would have called them the biggest bullshitter while laughing at the absurdity of it all.

Of course, reality had a way of bursting a girl's bubble. A notification popped up on my phone right then to remind me of the dreaded event happening this week. We had a court appearance scheduled in two days to testify in Shawna Miller's trial for breaking and entering Elijah's home.

Originally, when his ex-lover was found in the house, Elijah didn't want to press charges, and it was very confusing as to why. Eventually, after much cajoling, he'd finally shared his reasons.

Together with Grant and Rio, we'd thought of a major

hole in Shawna's blackmail scheme. Elijah had security cameras everywhere—and I meant everywhere. When she'd threatened to go public with photos of marks he or Grant left on her body after consensual rough sex, the entire conversation had been captured on film and audio.

The men had agreed to not press charges for attempted blackmail if she pleaded guilty to breaking and entering. And that big power play brought us to this hearing.

When we were first notified of the hearing, Elijah adamantly protested my attendance to his attorney. However, his objections were to no avail. I was being called as a witness, and so was he. Like it or not, we both had to be there.

About a week ago, we had been officially prepared by his attorney, and it seemed pretty cut-and-dry. He thought the trial would only last a day or two at the most, and she would get a slap on the wrist—community service and maybe a fine since nothing was stolen and no one was hurt. Not physically at least. We didn't bother bringing up the nightmares I had after that incident. I didn't want to give her the satisfaction of knowing she'd gotten to me. I would be glad when this was all put behind us.

Elijah was looking at his phone when I came into the bedroom. He must have just gotten the same notification since we shared the event on our calendars. When he met my eyes from across the room, his were filled with unspoken apology. He tossed his device onto the nightstand and came to me.

"Did you see that?" he asked quietly.

"Yeah. Somehow I'd put that out of my mind and had forgotten all about it until that notification came across my phone."

As if I were a treasured jewel, he ran his fingers reverently across my cheek. "I am so sorry you were ever exposed to that woman," he whispered, his full lips across mine. "I will live with that regret forever. If something had happened to you because of my careless ways—"

"Hey, hey. Stop this." I stopped his hand and held it while I spoke. "None of what happened was your fault. Clearly the woman has problems and couldn't separate reality from her fantasy. But that's not your fault. That has nothing to do with your actions. I don't want you blaming yourself for her irrational behavior. And look at me . . ." I waited for him to lift his eyes and meet my gaze. "I'm fine." I touched myself over my sternum with his hand in mine. And then repeated, "I'm fine."

He stared at me for what felt like an eternity. His beautiful, frosty-green eyes bored straight into my heart before he finally spoke again. "How did I get so lucky?" He kissed me softly but stopped before I could intensify the kiss. "I feel like something is going to happen to take you away from me. I've done too many bad things in my life to deserve someone as good as you."

"Elijah—"

"Please let me finish." My beautiful man dropped his chin to his chest and rested it there for a moment, seeming to need the time to collect himself. Pain began to strangle me, watching what he was putting himself through.

His chest expanded with his inhalation, and he lifted his face to my waiting attention. "I'm so scared your association with me is somehow going to cause you harm. That my punishment is going to be watching you suffer. It would be the absolute death of me." His Adam's apple bobbed as he swallowed around the thick emotion.

My voice was filled with anguish when I spoke. "Why are you saying all of this? What have you done that could possibly be so bad that you feel like you need to be punished? Will you tell me what is going on?" I begged him, and I could feel the tears welling in my eyes. Seeing him so emotional and hearing the pain in his voice was tearing my heart out.

"Maybe someday," he said and suddenly looked completely exhausted. "But right now, I want you in that shower, naked, in the next three minutes. I need to get lost in your body."

Well, what was I going to say to that? If that was what my man needed from me in that moment, that was what I would give him. All of me. Every time he asked. Everything he asked. Any way he asked. Because that was what a woman did for her man.

Right?

Again, sailing in uncharted waters here. But it seemed like the right thing to do. It felt like the right thing to do. He was telling me—in words—what he needed from me. What more could I ask from him?

There was a nagging voice arguing that he was burying an emotional burden with physical action, but I couldn't accuse him of something like that when the physical action was expressing love to each other. That seemed like complaining about winning the lottery because you enjoyed living paycheck to paycheck.

★ ★ ★

Two days later, we walked into a courtroom in the Van Nuys Courthouse. In recent years, Malibu was one of the smaller cities that fell victim to the countywide court consolidation in Los Angeles County. Therefore, the city no longer operated its own court system. Cases were now divided between this court and another courthouse near the airport.

The courtroom itself was much smaller than I expected and nothing like what you saw on television. It was much more like a conference room in a professional building, only bigger.

"Have you done something like this before?" I whispered to Elijah.

He looked so handsome in his gray suit and mint-green patterned tie. His eyes picked up the color in the tie like a sponge, and he was completely electrifying and mouthwatering. If I wasn't so damn nervous, I'd be all over the guy.

"I've been to court before, yes. I'm guessing you have not?" He gave me a lazy smile. How was he staying so relaxed through all of this?

I smoothed the kick pleat hemline on my gray dress one more time just to have something to do with my hands.

Elijah leaned closer to me and said right in my ear, "Stop fidgeting. You look gorgeous."

"I don't know why I'm so nervous. I haven't done anything wrong."

Our attorney was already waiting for us inside the room and motioned to chairs for us to sit. The proceedings got started soon after.

The district attorney walked into the room and took his place behind one of the chairs up front. Right behind him walked Shawna and her attorney, another beautiful woman about the same age.

Elijah sucked in a breath so harshly, I snapped my eyes in his direction. But even if I hadn't heard him inhale in surprise, his rigid posture would have caught my attention. Was he really that disturbed just by seeing this woman again?

"What in the actual fuck is going on here?" he muttered,

although it was so quiet I was sure no one else heard him but me.

Both women kept their eyes straight ahead toward the judge's bench.

The proceedings went as expected, and it was all over very quickly. As our attorney had prepared us, Shawna wasn't sentenced on the spot. Rather, the judge called for a recess and left the courtroom. People filed out into the hall to use the restroom, grab drinks, or just get some fresh air while we were on a break.

Elijah, on the other hand, took off for the door like the building was on fire. Nearly overturning my ankle because I wasn't used to wearing high heels and having to run after someone, I tried to keep up with him but lagged behind by at least five feet.

"My God, man, where's the damn fire? Can you slow down, please?"

When he turned around, he had such an agitated look on his face, I stopped in my tracks and reared back. "Whoa, okay. Do you need some time alone?" Honestly, he kind of scared me in his current state.

Immediately after seeing my reaction, his shoulders relaxed down to their normal position instead of ratcheted up near his ears with tension. He held his arms out to me, but I hesitated. The past few days, he had been more mercurial than I had ever known him to be, and it was confusing the hell out of me.

"Beauty, please. Come to me."

I stepped into his embrace and wrapped my arms around his waist. I could feel him trembling, so I insisted, "Tell me what is going on, and don't you dare say nothing. I swear I will leave right now." I pulled back out of his arms to look at him and waited for him to reply.

He swallowed roughly. You would think he'd had razor blades for lunch with the difficulty he had working his throat. Deep emotion was getting in the way of what he needed to tell me.

"Please. Try," I begged.

"The woman." He swallowed roughly again. "The attorney." Pause. "Shawna's attorney." Exhale. "That's my ex." Inhale. "Hensley." Swallow. "I don't know how the hell this could be happening." He added hand gestures then, raking both back through his thick hair and pulling on the ends. "I don't know what else to say. But my brain is so fucked up right now." He made eye contact finally and confessed to me—pleaded with me—like I could somehow make it better. "I looked for her. I looked for her for *years* after she ran out."

The way he emphasized that one word broke a piece of my heart clean off. He'd looked for an old girlfriend for years? Jesus, she must have really meant a lot to him.

"She left with my child inside her body and just fucking disappeared!" he yelled so loud, other people rerouted their walking path away from us.

Thunk.

Another piece—gone. They had a child together? He had a child with another woman and knew it and was playing house with me?

He was all but wailing up to the sky with his fist raised to the heavens, and I didn't know what to do. Go closer? Hug him? Punch him? I didn't think touching him seemed like a solid idea in that moment, so I let him pour it all out. I'd help him do damage control after his storm waters receded.

Maybe. Jury was still out on that one.

"And now she shows up here..." He pointed down to the ground. "On this day?"

Stab. Stab.

"She fucking shows up here? It doesn't make sense. It's too much of a coincidence." His voice drifted away with the passing cars.

Thankfully none of the pedestrians were paying him much mind now. I guess emotional outbursts weren't uncommon on the front steps of the courthouse. I had zero frame of reference. I had to get out of here, though. The things he'd just told me were bouncing around in my head, and all I could hear was *run, girl...*

Go! Run!

By some sort of miracle, a yellow taxi was among the next cluster of cars coming toward us. My hand went up of its own accord, and the car pulled to the curb. Elijah was so wrapped up in his own drama that it wasn't until the door slammed with me inside that he lifted his head and realized I was driving away.

I didn't look back.

CHAPTER SEVEN

ELIJAH

I knew it. I knew things were too good to last. How had all my searches come up empty while that little bitch was right in my backyard the whole time? But I had to keep my shit together and go back inside that courtroom and make sure justice was served for Hannah.

And what was that all about?

Did she get a call from her sister? Was her dad having another heart attack? She just got in that cab and drove away. Although, I had to admit, my head was so far up my own ass in that moment, she might have told me what was going on and I simply didn't remember.

"All right, man, get your shit together. One step at a time here." I muttered the encouragement to myself and rubbed the tension from my forehead. "Go back inside and listen to the sentence." I turned on my heel and started walking back toward the building. I felt like I was losing my damn mind. For fuck's sake, I was pacing in front of the county courthouse, talking to myself. And the craziest part of the entire scenario? Not a single passerby gave me a second look.

When these proceedings were over, I needed to call Bas and Grant. It was time to rally the troops. Hopefully their women would let them out on a weeknight.

As suspected, Shawna was given six months minus time served, which only amounted to about seventy-two hours for breaking and entering my home. Because she had a spotless record, extensive education, and long list of volunteer gigs in the community, her sentence was reduced to one year of court-approved community service less time served.

In other words, complete bullshit. I was kind of glad Hannah wasn't there to hear this in person. At least I could break it to her gently or sugarcoat it somehow. But where did she go?

I pulled out my phone and looked at the screen again, figuring she would have texted me by now to tell me what was going on, but the screen was still empty. No text messages, no voicemails, and not a single email from her either. This was not like her at all. Something was going on.

At least my two most threatening enemies to her were still in this room with me. Right where I could see them.

When I looked up, they were both staring at me, as if my thoughts had attracted their attention. But in reality, the last thing I wanted was attention from either of those two sirens. Shawna kept her eyes laser focused on me while leaning closer to Hensley and saying something exclusively for her ears.

My ex looked good. I'd be lying if I said she didn't. Like most females, pregnancy had left her with a woman's body. Delicious curves where there used to be none, and fuller, heavier breasts that advertised the woman was healthy and fertile.

Hensley let a devious smile—one I was much too familiar with—spread across her lips. A smile that ran the blood in my veins cold. I needed to get out of this courtroom as fast as possible.

Unfortunately, my attorney wanted to chitchat about everything and anything. Because the guy was getting paid by the hour, and it was in his best interest to drag out every single meeting we had.

With a hearty pat on the back, I leaned into the guy. "Hey, man, I really appreciate everything you've done for us on this case, but I need to get going. Something has come up with Hannah, and I need to meet up with her."

"I was wondering what happened to her," he said. "I hope everything is okay."

"Me too. Thank you again. Please send all the bills to my office. Not a single one to Hannah. I'll be taking care of everything. Have a great day." I shook his hand one last time before making a beeline toward the exit.

Cell phone already in hand, I hit the speed dial for Hannah's number and put the phone to my ear. The call rang straight through to her voicemail. With a frown, I checked the display and disconnected the call. Then redialed. Two, three, four rings, and voicemail again. This time I decided to leave a message, and I was sure I sounded winded as I bounced down the concrete stairs in front of the building.

"Hey, beauty, it's me. Where did you go? Call me back please so I can meet up with you." I disconnected the call and made sure my ringer was on one more time, since I had turned it off for the court proceedings. I dashed out a quick text to Lorenzo and let him know I was ready to be picked up in front of the building and then stashed my phone inside my suit jacket. I would call my buddies from inside the car.

While I waited for my driver, I heard a familiar feminine voice behind me. Just not the one I wanted to hear. Every hair on my neck stood on end, and not from arousal.

"Elijah. Do you have a minute?" Hensley Pritchett—in the flesh—stood beside me on the sidewalk.

"For you? No, not really."

"Oh, come on. Don't be like that." She reached out to put her hand on mine, and I moved out of her grasp. Hurt filled her eyes while her other features fell with sadness.

Well, tough shit, wasn't it? If she knew half the time I spent hurting because of her, she'd be a little more gracious about taking one measly comment for the team.

"I was hoping you would meet me here for dinner." She handed me a business card from a small restaurant near Shark Enterprises. "I've made reservations for seven." She put her hand up in a stop gesture. "Don't answer now. Just show up or don't. But I think we have some things to discuss."

"I'm with someone now," I blurted for no reason at all.

"Good. You should bring her. We can swap stories. You know"—she looked at me slyly—"maybe of your childhood and stuff." She blew me a kiss and sauntered off toward the parking garage.

God, how I wished I was behind the wheel of a moving vehicle right then. It would be so easy to just mow her down, throw it in reverse, and hit her again. Maybe drive forward one last time for good measure as I escaped the scene of the crime. I mean, what the hell, right? I already had one murder on my conscience. What was one more? Once your soul was damned, it's damned, as far as I could figure.

Lorenzo picked me up moments after she disappeared. I called Hannah at least five more times by the time we got to Shark Enterprises.

"Usual time today, boss?" my faithful driver asked.

"Actually, it looks like I have dinner plans here in

downtown. Can you leave a car in the parking structure for me sometime today? That way you don't have to stay on the clock too late."

"Yeah, sure, I can do that. But you know I don't mind. That's what you pay me for." He said the last bit with a laugh, but honestly, my mood had taken a nosedive, so I just got out of the car and, with purposeful strides, made it to the front door.

Once upstairs at my office, I was surprised to see a female at Carmen's desk.

"Oh, hi there," she purred.

"Hello," I said curiously. "Where's the man who usually sits at this desk?"

"I'm not really sure. The agency just tells me where to report and what the job will be. They don't really tell me why the person is absent from work." She raked her gaze up and down my body, and I shivered. Just that look made me want to take a shower.

"I see. Well, this is my office. Hopefully you've been able to make heads or tails of my schedule there." I tapped my finger on the computer monitor. "I don't think I have anything particularly challenging today besides the appointment I just came from, so it should be a pretty routine day. And I'm sorry. I didn't get your name?"

The pretty woman stood and offered her hand. "I'm so sorry. My name is Gina. Just let me know what I can do to help you, Mr. Banks."

After shaking her hand, I went into my office and closed the door. I called Lorenzo because I was running out of options.

"Yes, Mr. Banks, how can I help you? Did you leave something in the car?"

"No, but I'm hoping you can help me. I'm having trouble

getting a hold of Hannah. Can you look on the car's phone history and see if there are any numbers for her family members? Maybe her parents or her sisters?"

"Oh, yes, of course. Give me one second. Actually, let me hang up, and I'll check. I think it will be quicker if I'm not connected to the system. I think she usually uses her own phone, but I'll look. I will text you if I find anything, okay?"

"Yeah, sure. That's great. I'll look for your text." I threw my phone onto my desk—probably a little harder than I should have—then quickly picked it back up to make sure I didn't just break anything vital . . . and then set it down more gently. I fell into my chair and let it roll back a little from the desk and tried to remember what Hannah had said to me before she got into that cab.

I remember being agitated about seeing Hensley. But I thought I was just ranting and raving about the unexpectedness of that and how I had been searching for her and being frustrated that I'd searched for years for that woman and she'd somehow managed to elude me.

Was that it?

Was it admitting I'd searched for years? Did I sound obsessed? Like a stalker? Oh, shit. Oh, shit. Shit. No. No . . . no! I'd said she'd had my baby inside her.

It all came flooding back. I could see the whole scene playing out in front of me like I was watching a movie. I heard the words come out of my mouth and saw the look on her face in reaction. I scrubbed my face with my palms and shot to my feet. How the hell was this happening? For one thing, how was Hensley back in Los Angeles and none of my contacts alerted me? And how the hell did I temporarily lose my shit about it in front of Hannah? Well, I wouldn't be shocked if I'd just destroyed the best thing I ever had in my life.

Out of habit, I picked up the phone and hit the button to call Grant. His assistant, Reina, picked up after two rings.

"Good afternoon. Grant Twombley's office. This is Reina."

"Good afternoon, Reina. Is the tall guy around? This is Elijah Banks."

"Good afternoon, Mr. Banks. I believe he's in Mr. Shark's office. Do you want me to patch you through?"

"No, thank you. I'll just walk down there. I could use some fresh air. Thank you." I hung up the phone and rested my head back on the chair. *Jesus Christ, what have I done?* I knew I had at least three emails that needed attention, though, before I could go worry about my personal life.

I brought my computer to life, typed in my password, and opened my email. Maybe I could try to get some work done. As usual, those three emails led to two monumental problems, and only one had an immediate solution.

By the time I was finished doing damage control, most of the building had gone home for the day. If I were going to make it to my dinner appointment with my ex, I needed to get on my way. Earlier, Lorenzo messaged that a car was waiting for me in the parking structure, and I sent Gina downstairs to the security desk to pick up the key.

Before I pulled out, I looked at the card again to make sure I had the address correct. I punched it into the navigation assistant in the car and followed the directions to the restaurant.

From the moment I walked in, I didn't like the layout. Romantic tables were set up in a very dimly lit dining room, and almost every table had only two place settings.

What was this woman playing at? Well, she was in for

a rude awakening if she thought she was going to catch my interest ever again. No matter what she was trying to pull, she wouldn't get away with it.

I gave the hostess my name and told her who I was meeting, and she efficiently showed me to the table where Hensley was already waiting. She wore a bloodred cocktail dress with a plunging neckline, not the suit she'd worn in court today. When the hell did she have time to go home and change? And did it really matter? I certainly wasn't going to compliment her on her appearance. She had always been a very shallow girl and insecure about her looks. But those weren't my problems anymore.

When she began to stand as I approached the table, I held my hand out. "No, please stay seated," I said and quickly took my seat so we wouldn't attract attention. The last thing I needed was to be seen here with this woman. I still hadn't been able to get ahold of Hannah before coming here, and if for some reason she found out about this before I was able to tell her, it would look bad. Really bad.

"I'm so glad you could make it," Hensley cooed.

"Save the niceties and just get to the point. What do you want to talk to me about?" I kept my tone curt.

"Let's order drinks," she said. "Still a Scotch man?" she inquired as the waitress approached our table.

"I'm driving tonight, so I'll just have an iced tea, please," I said to the server.

Hensley frowned dramatically, and honestly, I'd forgotten how ridiculous this girl could be with her pageantry. "Oh, you're no fun." She pouted and took a playful swipe at my hand.

I moved both hands into my lap so she wouldn't be tempted to try to touch me again. She noticed my movement but didn't comment, but I could see the hurt in her eyes. She always did have a shitty poker face.

After turning her attention to the waitress, she asked for a glass of the house cab. With a polite smile, the server hurried off to get our drinks, and we were left alone once more.

She leaned forward on her forearms, thrusting her breasts up and toward me in a calculated maneuver while she spoke. I made sure to keep my eyes locked on hers the entire time. She needed to get the message that every game she played, I would shut down on the first move.

"It's so good to see you," Hensley offered quietly. "You really look good."

"What did you want to see me about? Why did you ask me to meet you?"

"Can't we visit a little bit first? Don't treat me like I'm a stranger. There was a time you said I was the love of your life." Hensley arranged and rearranged her silverware while she spoke.

"Well, I was wrong."

"So, the girl you were with today, the blonde? Is she the love of your life currently? Because my client was under the impression *she* was. Isn't it funny how all the women you get involved with end up thinking that?" Hensley stared at me after laying down that mouthful.

I'd promised myself I wouldn't take her bait. I wouldn't fight with this woman in public or cause a scene in any way. From the moment I'd agreed to this meeting, I'd had to keep reminding myself of all those promises to ensure none of those things happened. I didn't need that kind of publicity, and neither did Hannah. If nothing else, that was what motivated me most. Hannah. So I just sat and glared across the table, waiting for this evil woman to get to the point.

Our waitress returned with our drinks and took our dinner order. I stuck with something quick and light because there was a good chance I wasn't going to be eating it anyway. If I made it that far into this meeting, it would be a small miracle.

"So how are Sebastian and Grant? I'm assuming the three of you are still thick as thieves?" She smiled when she asked about my best friends.

"They're both really good. That's all you need to know."

"I'm glad to hear that." She kept her eyes fixed on me while she said it, determined to convince me it was genuine. Didn't she understand I would never believe another word out of her mouth as long as I lived?

"Why are you here? Back in LA, I mean?" If she wouldn't get to the point, I would. I really was not interested in a social call with this woman.

"I grew up here. This is my home. You know that. Plus, I got a really good job offer with the city. I couldn't turn it down. It really made the most sense." She shrugged like it was just that easy. Like she didn't rip my heart out when she ran off with another man while pregnant with my child. Oh, minor details . . . so easy to forget.

"Then why did you leave in the first place? If you had such deep roots in your hometown?"

"To go to law school. And to have help with the baby while I did that. I went and stayed with my mom in Chicago."

"I would've helped you," I snarled through gritted teeth. And what the fuck? I thought her mother lived here in Los Angeles. Just another lie. But it didn't matter at this point. None of it did.

"Don't start, okay?" she implored calmly. "I really just

wanted to catch up. Not rehash old arguments."

"What did you think would happen? I know that child is mine. I looked everywhere for you, so I know you were intentionally trying to not be found. I have a right to know my own child, Hensley," I said in a low, lethal voice. I couldn't help the anger that seethed from my heart when I thought of how many years of my child's life I'd already been denied.

"He's not yours, Elijah. I've said it before. I'm not trying to hurt you with that information, but it's the truth," she said in a sympathetic tone while reaching out to touch my hand atop the table.

Swiftly I moved it out of reach.

"The timing doesn't line up. I've been over it and over it. There's just no way…" I drifted off. I didn't know what else to say. She was right. The pain was as fresh as if it had just happened ten minutes ago. If she had been unfaithful and made a life—a fucking life—with another man while living with me and then led me to believe it was my child for months until she couldn't take the guilt anymore—it was the lowest thing a woman could do to a man.

"I want a paternity test. I'll take it to the courts if I have to." My hurt quickly morphed to anger, as it so often did when I thought about this situation. I didn't have a trick to quell my rage on the topic, either. No breathing technique or mantra could bring me down from the adrenaline spike lashing my system.

"I don't want to have to leave the area again, but I will if it comes to that," she said with resignation. "Please don't force my hand."

"Why would you have to leave the area? If he's not my child, you have nothing to worry about, right?" I stared at her

VICTORIA BLUE

for a few long moments, then finally said, "The fact that you would even consider running again tells me you're not sure who the father is. For one thing, it makes me sick and really pisses me off that you were cheating on me. I gave you everything. Every fucking thing. But more importantly, I'm determined to find out if the child is mine, because I deserve to be a part of his life if he is."

"I didn't want to have to do this, but you're going to leave me no choice," she said through gritted teeth.

Ahhh, here came the woman I knew.

"Do what?"

"I'll expose your dirty laundry if I hear another word about a paternity test. So help me God, Elijah, I will. I'm not going to have my child's world split in two while he's shuffled from household to household." She sat back and drained her glass of wine in one gulp.

There was no way I was going to sit here and enjoy a friendly meal with this bitch. I stood up while reaching in my back pocket for my wallet. I couldn't even stand the thought of being indebted to her for the drink I only half consumed. While preoccupied with the task, someone approached the table from behind.

"Elijah? Is that you?" a vaguely familiar female voice questioned.

When I turned to see who was standing behind me, I was shocked to see Hannah's younger sister Sheppard standing there, looking mighty proud of herself, if I was reading her posture correctly.

For Christ's sake, could this night get any worse?

It took me a few beats to organize my thoughts into a coherent sentence and pull my facial expression into one

137

that wasn't full of frustration. Or guilt. Because I wasn't doing anything wrong, goddammit.

"Hey, Sheppard, how are you?" I nearly choked on the question.

I was still seething from Hensley's rant, and now this. I didn't know the young woman well enough to pull her in for so much as a friendly hug, so I stood there awkwardly, not knowing what to do with my hands. Shoving them into my pockets seemed like the best option.

"I didn't mean to interrupt your"—she paused there, assessing Hensley and then the romantic table setting for two, and then roamed her eyes up and down my frame—"date?"

"Oh, this is not a date," I said with way too much insistence and volume for the setting. I physically winced and remodulated my voice. "More of a business meeting."

Sheppard just nodded through my stammering and kept her shrewd eyes fixed on mine, definitely not buying my story and not offering an out by way of a conversational shift either.

After an eternity of uncomfortable silence, she said, "Well, I'll let Hannah know I saw you tonight. I'm sure she'll be happy to hear I ran into you. And I'm sorry"—here she plastered on the cheerleader smile I'd seen Hannah deploy so many times—"what did you say your name was?" The twin thrust her hand in Hensley's face to shake.

Taken aback by her forwardness, Hensley automatically offered her hand in response and said, "I'm Hensley Pritchett. It's so nice to meet you. Enjoy your dinner. I love this place."

"Oh, thank you. This is my first time here. It looks lovely, though. Very romantic." Sheppard widened her eyes comically and gave a little shimmy as though she were so excited to be on her own date. "I'm really sorry I interrupted you two. I'll get out of your way now. Bye." She threw one last glare in my direction, thrust her hand into her waiting date's, and strolled off toward their table.

Hensley chuckled. "Another heart you broke, I'm guessing by the daggers she was shooting you?"

"No," I grumbled. "That's Hannah's sister, and she's probably texting her right now telling her that she saw me here with another woman. Fuck me, seriously. This night just keeps getting better and better." I rubbed my forehead in frustration. I'd be lucky if my beauty ever spoke to me again after this. To my ex, I said, "This isn't over." And I nearly knocked our waitress down as I stormed out of the restaurant.

I didn't want to hear her response or give her an opportunity to say anything more. I just needed to get out of there and call Hannah and do as much damage control as I could—maybe even before her sister got in touch with her. And of all the sisters to run into, it had to be that one.

Sheppard would take delight in hurting Hannah with traitorous news. And I was the bastard who'd loaded the weapon and handed it to her with the safety off.

The windshield in my car fogged while I sat staring at the dashboard, trying to figure out my plan of attack. Every way I thought of turning seemed like a brick wall or a viper's pit. For fuck's sake, how had I gotten myself into this predicament? Oh, that's right. Fucking Hensley Pritchett. Of course! I should've known better than to meet her without telling Hannah about it first.

Hitting the programmed name on my phone, I waited for the call to connect. I was in no shape to drive until I had some sort of mental clarity, so waiting for the defroster to clear the glass in front of my face wasn't a hardship.

"Where the fuck have you been all day?" Grant said in greeting when he picked up.

"You won't believe the day I've had, man," I said, and I swear it came out close to a whimper as I rested my forehead on the steering wheel. A fucking *whimper*. "Can you get away for a bit?"

"You okay, my brother? You don't sound so good." My best friend's tone shifted from his typical upbeat razz to immediate concern.

"No." I sighed so heavily, the windshield immediately clouded up again. "No, I'm not. I fucked up big time, and I don't know how to fix it."

"Where are you? Stay put, and I'll come to you. I'm at the downtown condo. Are you close?"

"Yeah," I huffed. "I'm actually sitting in my car a few blocks from SE."

"Do you want me to loop Bas in? Three heads are better than two and all that? Why don't we meet up top?"

Grant was referring to our modern-day clubhouse we'd been frequenting up on the rooftop of the building the Shark's Edge offices were in. A little more than a month back, Sebastian's sister, Pia, arranged a comfortable secret hangout for us.

"Yeah, that's a solid plan, actually. And dude?"

"Shit, Banks, you're freaking me out, not gonna lie right now," Grant vowed solemnly.

"Just bring the Lagavulin," I requested while rubbing my forehead. The stress of the evening—no, the entire day—was throbbing at my temples and radiating across my frontal lobe by that point.

"Oh, hell. Sit tight, my brother. I'll see if I can wrangle

Shark, and we'll meet up top in less than thirty. Do you need me to come find you, or are you good to get there?"

"Nah, I'll see you up there. Like I said, I'm just blocks away. Think I'll hoof it, though. The movement might do me some good." I exhaled fully for the first time possibly all day. Before the line was cut, I said, "Grant?"

"Yeah, man?"

"Thank you. I mean it."

"I got you."

Deciding it was safe enough to leave my car where it was, I locked the doors and walked several blocks south to the building where we were meeting. I showed the night security guard my identification and took the elevator to the roof. I was the first one to arrive, and I walked to the edge to look out over the city. It was a stunning view from up here. High enough to feel insulated from the hassles of society but not so high that you weren't reminded there was life throbbing right below you in the streets.

Overall, it was exactly what I needed. To take a step back and look at the day, look at the events of the day, because so much had happened in the past twelve hours, it was hard to digest while in the thick of it.

When I asked myself the vital question, *Did it matter to me if things worked out with Hannah?*, the answer was unequivocally yes. Every single time. Yes. In fact, I couldn't think of anything that mattered to me more.

I still didn't trust Hensley. I didn't think I could ever trust that woman again. But the fact remained, I had the right to know if I was the father of her child. I had a right to know the child, too. Neither of those two things were negotiable in my mind and, more importantly, in my heart.

By that point, I surmised that the child was a boy, and I had personal experience with what growing up fatherless did to a young boy and young man. I wouldn't wish that on my worst enemy. Hell, even if the child wasn't mine, if there was a way to somehow nurture the boy without giving his mother the wrong idea, I would do it.

Knowing Hannah and the kind of family ties she had, I felt pretty certain she would support me on all those decisions, too. I just had to have the opportunity to talk to her about the situation.

Behind me, I heard the elevator door open, and Sebastian and Grant's conversation spread across the quiet rooftop like a blanket of fog. Low and lush, their baritone voices were a dull hum until they were close enough for me to discern individual words.

Why I was gifted with these two men in my life, I would never know. But I was so grateful to see them I could have wept. Not that I did—talk about the quickest way to have Bas run for an exit. Hell, he might even dive right over the side of the building. Even though his tolerance for emotional displays had loosened up since meeting Abbigail and especially since their son arrived, he still avoided discussing feelings like the plague.

After the compulsory round of handshakes, backslaps, and bro hugs, Grant thumped the bottle of Scotch in the center of the low coffee table.

Bas gave me a skeptical glance. "How bad is it? Do we need a shot before we hear what dragged us out here?"

"Couldn't hurt," I said with my hands deep in my trouser pockets. I wasn't ready to dive into the nightmare just yet.

Grant grabbed the glasses from the cabinet built into the

coffee table—seriously, Pia thought of everything with this sun deck design—and poured us each a drink.

I held my glass toward the center of our group and said, "To women." My best friends tapped my glass with theirs, and we threw our heads back and shot our drinks in one gulp. I followed the motion through and slumped down until my head rested on the back cushion of the sofa. Then I just sat there for a few minutes with my eyes closed and enjoyed the burn of the Scotch until my stomach was warm from the alcohol.

Christ, no wonder my dad was a drunk. That feeling was heavenly. Especially after a day like the one I'd had. With his temperament, I think most of his days were difficult ones.

But honestly, that motherfucker was the last person I wanted to be thinking about at the moment. I sighed loudly and sat up, reaching for the bottle.

Grant shot out his long arm and stopped me. Only turning my head, I stared at him and nearly growled, "What?"

"Talk."

I continued the staredown, but it was getting me nowhere. Other than pissing me off, I couldn't figure out why the guy was stopping me from catching a buzz.

"Seriously, man, you didn't round us up to watch you get shitfaced. What's going on?" Grant let his hand slide off the bottle and sat back in his chair but never took his blue eyes off me.

"I saw Hensley today." There. He wanted me to talk, I talked. What more did I need to say to these two? They knew everything that woman stood for in my life. All the poisonous lies and evil manipulations she used to gut me. They'd had to bear witness to it all. They'd watched me go from a strong, productive, confident man . . . to a shell.

Because of her.

If anyone wouldn't need further explanation of what just seeing that woman would do to me, it would be these two men.

"Fuck me," Grant said and gripped the back of his neck.

"That's a Benji, Twombley." Bas held his flat palm out as if to collect a debt from Grant.

"Yeah, yeah."

"Oh, this is precious." I scowled at their antics. "You two assholes are betting on my worst nightmare now? Awesome."

Grant folded his wallet and stuffed it back in his pocket. "It's not like that. Don't get all butthurt. On our way over here, we were speculating what this could be about." He took a slow drink and then asked, "So where did she park her broom? I thought the sky looked a bit darker around midday. Must have been when she flew into town."

Bas stuffed the hundred into his billfold and put his wallet away while Grant was talking. I couldn't help but be annoyed about their bet, but truth be told, if the shoe were on the other foot, I would've done the same thing, so I shook it off.

"Well? Where did you see her?" Bas asked, already growing impatient. He never had liked the woman. Even when things were good between us.

"You are not going to believe this." I shook my head, still finding it all too coincidental. I slammed my second drink and waited for the burn to clear from my throat.

"Hannah and I had to be in court this morning for the breaking-and-entering case against Shawna. And guess who her attorney was?"

Grant snapped his head to look my way. "You can't be serious."

"Oh, I'm very serious. There's nothing about that woman

I find remotely humorous. Trust me."

"Shit. What did Hannah do?" Grant asked but immediately answered his own question. "Well, nothing, I suppose. She wouldn't know who that woman was unless you were stupid enough to tell her," Grant narrated, as if telling the story of my day. Or at least my day in a perfect world.

"Dude. Tell us you didn't do that," Bas added.

Both men froze in place, hanging on my next words.

Shaking my head, I said, "No. I didn't have to."

"That...little," Grant said as if each word was its own sentence. As if separating each individual word would highlight its specific gravity and therefore its value in his statement.

"Bitch," Sebastian finished, whether for effect or impatience, I couldn't tell, but I was the first to vocally agree.

With a curt nod, I said, "My thoughts exactly. Christ, it felt like seeing a ghost."

They both kept their eyes fixed on me like I was a grenade with the pin pulled. Then, they looked at each other, maybe trying to decide who would dive on the thing to save the city below from the impending explosion. Because after all these years of anxiously threatening how that woman would rue the day she came face-to-face with me again, they were expecting an emotional display of epic proportion.

Shit. Those were just the threats I made out loud. If anyone was privy to the dark ideas that ran through my mind on a frequent, evil loop? I probably would have had the room next to Rio Gibson's at that fancy little loony bin Grant sprang her from.

"You good, Banks?" Grant choked out.

His words shook me from the darkness. And I wasn't talking about the rooftop ambiance. But it jolted me back to regaling them with the day's events.

"And then!" My voice went up about two octaves in tone, and my agitation blasted the volume way past conversational. "Then!" I repeated just as loud, this time rocking on the balls of my feet like an attorney objecting to a judge's ruling. "She asked me to meet her for dinner!"

I waited for my buddies' outraged input, but they both stared at me like they were still waiting for the story's climax. So I charged on.

"And Hannah was already gone. She just got in a cab and drove away. And now she's been ghosting me all day." I wearily fell back into my seat and rested my elbows on my knees and my face in my palms.

"Oh, shit. Not good," Grant commiserated. "That's never good."

I dragged my hands down my forlorn face and looked at my best friends. The weight of the entire day settled on my shoulders and cramped the muscles in my neck.

"Yeah, tell me about it. That girl is so true. So honest—to her very soul. I'm so scared I fucked things up with her," I mumbled and hung my head.

Bas had been characteristically quiet. His pacing was on brand too. The man was a Socratic thinker, we always teased. If he was moving on the outside, his gears were moving on the inside as well.

"Back up the broomstick for a minute," the guy said and came to a halt. He narrowed his eyes while staring at me for a few uncomfortable moments. "These dots aren't connecting for me."

Instantly I felt defensive. "What's to connect, man? My lying, cheating ex is back in town, and apparently the woman

I'm in love with can't handle it and is now ghosting me." I rubbed the tense muscle in my forehead, trying to relax at least marginally. I was going to need Botox injections by the time I cleared up this mess.

"Dude. None of this makes sense. Everyone has exes. Shit, you've had your cock in half the city at this point. She's okay with that, but one legit girlfriend crawls out from under whatever rock she's been hiding, and that's what sends her running? Doesn't add up." Sebastian gave his head a little shake like he was swiping away a pesty gnat and looked to Twombley for some backup.

"You gonna say anything over there? Or are you just window dressing tonight?" He knocked Grant's knee with the toe of his dress shoe.

Does this man ever wear casual clothes?

"Yeah, I'm trying to make sense of all of it myself," Grant said. He gave me a shrewd head-to-toe scan before saying, "Don't think we missed the"—he made air quotes—"*woman I'm in love with* comment. I'm just waiting to unpack that gift and give it the full attention it deserves."

Bas chuckled. "Shit, right? Don't get me wrong, I couldn't be happier for you, man. Just hearing that someone has possibly reignited that level of emotion in you again is worth finishing that whole bottle in celebration." He gestured toward the Scotch on the low table in front of Grant.

"So why are we here watching you drown in misery instead? It seems like there's something you're not telling us," Grant subtly accused.

"I've gone over it again and again and again," I admitted and cringed when I figuratively stepped back and heard myself in this conversation. I sounded like a whining pussy, and it wasn't a part I took pride in playing.

Bas cut me off. "No way. Not you."

For that he got a glare and the head tilt, but I held back the expletive I wanted to spit in his direction. Especially after my own self-evaluation of the situation. Instead, I poured us all another drink and promptly consumed mine in one long chug. Finally, I was starting to feel more from the Scotch than just the burn in my throat.

Both of my friends cringed while watching me, and I scowled. "When did the two of you become so judgmental? You're like a bunch of nagging women."

My own comment made me take pause. Before this incident, I would have thought Hannah Farsey was the least judgmental person I had ever met. Yet here I was, alone, when I could have really used her support. However, upon hearing one fact she didn't like the sound of, she ran away.

Facing that character flaw in her was one of the hardest parts of today. No, not one of—it was the single worst. I had put her up so high on a pedestal, and she just knocked herself down a notch or two, and it sucked watching her fall.

I still thought she was the closest thing to perfect I would ever know, but I couldn't help but feel a twinge of disappointment. I'd like to think if the shoe were on the other foot, I'd at least hear her out. I didn't even know where she was staying, or I would just show up at her doorstep and insist we talk this out.

"So did you just want us to sit and admire your model good looks while you think things through, or are you going to let us help you?" Grant asked. "I mean, you are pretty and all that shit the ladies say, but you know that doesn't fly with me." He nodded toward Sebastian. "And I don't think Abbi is into sharing him, so those days are done for the two of you."

Bas glared at Grant. "Shut the fuck up," he growled, shaking his head, but I didn't miss the way the corner of his mouth was fighting not to rise in a grin.

"Was anything said about the baby? Or child by now. Christ, how long has it been—three . . . no, five years?"

"Would you believe it's been six?"

"That's crazy."

"It really is. And yes, when I asked her about the child, she continued to deny I'm the father. I told her I wanted a paternity test done, and she said no."

"Well, it's not going to be up to her," Bas said. "I mean, you're still going to pursue it, right? Now that you know where she is, you can have a court-ordered test. I think there are attorneys who specialize in this very thing." Sebastian finally sat down but leaned forward with his elbows on his knees, never relaxing while he spoke. I wasn't sure if it was his new trip down Fatherhood Lane that had him so invested in this topic or if he really hated Hensley that much. Any way he could see her burn would be good enough in his mind.

"What's up, man?" Grant zeroed in on my discomfort. While Sebastian focused on what people said and what he was going to say in response, Grant typically focused on their body language and their emotional tells. It was why they made such a powerful team in business. They were the perfect one-two punch.

"I keep getting hung up on the same thing. I mean, fuck . . ." I gave my head a little shake and chuckled. Although there wasn't a single thing funny about this situation. When no one spoke, I looked up and saw both of my best friends' eyes on me, both silently supporting me and encouraging me to get what was bothering me off my chest. Again. Just like they had been our entire friendship.

"If that child is not mine, that means she was cheating on me. I just can't wrap my head around that. I know I've had a long time to build up serious ill will toward that woman, but it wasn't always that way. When we were happy, we were really happy." I traced the rim of the glass with my finger just to do something with the nervous energy still coursing through my system.

"It's hard to look back on that time and try to figure out where it went wrong. You know? Like what did I do wrong? Where did I come up short? I really thought I was a great boyfriend. When she told me she was pregnant, I thought we were both over the moon with happiness and excitement."

I was on a roll now. It was like the floodgates had opened and I couldn't stop talking. "And do you want to know something even crazier? I feel bad for the other guy. That's ridiculous, right? I actually feel bad for the guy who knocked up my girlfriend because she was playing that dude too. I mean, think about it. He's in the exact same shitty situation I am. He doesn't know if that's his kid or not."

Grant's face twisted with objection, and I could tell he didn't want to say what he was thinking.

We all knew each other way too long to pull any punches with each other, so I goaded him, "Just say what you need to say, my brother. I'm not going to break into pieces here."

"Not this time, at least," Bas mumbled into his glass.

"Well, you don't know what situation he's in. He may not even know that she had a child, or a boyfriend at the time." Grant threw his arms up to accentuate his point. But when you're six-and-a-half-feet tall, your arms are more like the wingspan of a Boeing 737, and clearance from the nearest air traffic control tower must first be obtained.

Bas and I both ducked and narrowly missed being clipped by his exuberant arm gestures.

"Hell, there may not even be another guy. She could be lying about that. Just because she wasn't with you when she walked out doesn't mean she was with someone else."

"You make a solid point, Twombley," Bas conceded and stretched a fist toward the big guy to bump.

"Hold up, hold up. Before you start celebrating too much, I haven't gotten to the worst part yet."

I really should have had my camera at the ready to capture their reaction. In tandem, both Grant and Bas turned their heads in my direction and said, "What?"

That one word came at me in stereo with one voice just a fraction of a second behind the other, so it sounded more like an echo. *"Wha-What?"*

"Hard to believe, isn't it? That this mess can get even bigger? Messier?"

"Well, lay it on us. Rip the damn Band-Aid off already."

"I decided to meet Hensley for dinner. I mean, what the hell, right? How much worse could the day get?" I said, trying to play it off like I hadn't been shitting bricks the whole time leading up to that fiasco.

"Why does this feel like you agreed to go into the belly of the beast? I mean, already, without hearing any other details . . . ?" Grant asked, his light brows hiked all the way up to meet where his hair flopped across the middle of his forehead.

"Because at this point, agreeing to do anything involving that woman feels like making a deal with the devil himself."

CHAPTER EIGHT

HANNAH

"Hey, I didn't expect to see you here today," my boss and friend Rio Gibson said when I walked in the door of Abstract Catering's prep kitchen in Inglewood. It was after regular working hours, and I'd taken a chance that she would still be here. I'd already walked around my favorite mall, hoping some retail therapy would clear my head.

It hadn't.

Then I'd taken another Uber to this location in hopes that my friend would still be here. She had mentioned staying late to work on the mountain of paperwork on her desk.

"To be honest, I didn't expect to be here either." My cheerleader smile was firmly in place, but I winced when I heard the snarky tone in my voice. Rio didn't deserve that. Hell, no one did.

"Everything okay?" She scanned me from head to toe with shrewd eyes. This woman didn't miss a trick. Rio would make a great mom one day, with her finely tuned bullshit meter, keen eye, and enormous, generous heart. Reminded me a lot of my own mom, actually.

"Yeah." I sighed heavily and probably gave myself away with that prolonged exhale. "Okay, fine. Not really. Elijah and I got into a fight, and I stormed off. Now I don't have a car because mine is at his house. Is there any chance I can borrow Kendall?" I winced and wished I could retract into my shoulders like a turtle did into its shell to escape the awkwardness of having to ask for help. It wasn't a predicament I liked being in.

"Of course! I'll get the keys. But you may have to put gas in her." She cringed like she was breaking bad news. "I think she's pretty close to empty. I was planning on filling up on my way home this afternoon."

"Are you fairly certain Grant will be able to come by and pick you up?" I asked, taking the keys for the Fiat. "I can hang tight if you want to get in touch with him. I don't want to leave you stranded."

"Well, coincidentally," she said with a sly grin, "he already messaged and told me that he was going out with the guys tonight. So, if you want some company?" She let the words hang in the air for a few beats and then finished her thought, "I'm free."

"I'm afraid I'm not going to be very good company tonight."

"Oh, don't be ridiculous. Do you remember the way you listened to me cry for hours when Grant was missing? I think I owe you some shoulder time, girlfriend."

"Rio, we've talked about this before. Girlfriends don't punch clocks when it comes to time spent supporting each other."

"I know, I know. You're right. Don't forget"—she waved her hand wildly while she made an excuse for herself—"I'm new to all these matters of the heart and whatnot." She finished the statement with a prolonged eye roll and slight head shake just in case I didn't understand what she really thought about messy feelings.

"Could've fooled me. You've taken to it like a champ." I knocked my shoulder into hers, and my friend was so lightweight I almost knocked her off her feet. True, I also had some pent-up aggression, and I might have knocked into her a little too hard. "Sorry. I didn't mean to bump you so hard. But do you see what I'm talking about? I don't think I'm safe to be on the streets right now."

"Well, what are your plans for tonight? I don't think you should just sit home alone." Rio shut down her computer and gave me her full attention.

"I'm not sure. Now that I have a car again, I may drive up the coast a little bit and then turn around and come back. Sometimes just driving really clears my head."

Rio nodded while I was talking. "I get that, I do. But sometimes for anxious girls like you"—she poked her index finger into my chest then thumbed back to her own—"and me, being alone with our thoughts is some of the worst time spent."

Well, shit, she wasn't wrong. And damn it, why did she have to mention it now? Couldn't she see I was trying to run away from my problems? Not face them head on. *How mentally healthy and responsible can one girl be in a day?*

A ridiculous giggle bubbled up in the back of my throat, and I nearly choked because it quickly turned on me and became a hairball of emotions I really—and I did mean really—didn't feel equipped to deal with at the moment. But I also couldn't continue to deny her assertion straight to her face. Because then not only would I be a head case, but I'd be a delusional head case to boot.

"Well, I've said my piece. You know where to find me if you need an ear, or a shoulder, or someone to help you dig a deep, deep hole, okay?" Rio gave me a cheeky wink and yanked me close for a hug.

I really was incredibly lucky to have this woman in my life. She wasn't much older than me, but she had enough years on me to be an excellent mentor and role model but was still close enough in age to be completely relatable and fun.

"Woman . . . I think I love you!" I said to her and disengaged from the hug we were sharing.

"I definitely love you, pretty girl," she said with a gentle smile while stroking my hair away from my face. It was such a motherly gesture, I could feel the emotion ball moving up in my throat again.

Thank God Rio always knew just where to inject some humor. We both took a step back as she issued instructions. "Now, go clean your chakras or whatever, and take good care of my sweet baby, Kendall."

"She's in good hands, I promise."

"Good. See to it. Because apparently the universe is determined to ensure that's the closest I ever come to parenthood." My pixie friend rolled her eyes like she so often did and, this time, exhaled in a huff from her bottom lip so her bangs pulled a Marilyn Monroe.

"Can we unpack this? Did something happen?" I leaned against Abbigail's desk and focused on Rio completely. Since I'd been working here, this woman had given me so much of her time and attention. The least I could do was stop and listen to her when she clearly was laying out breadcrumbs from a conversational loaf she wanted to break with someone.

Of course, just as quickly, she clammed up. She went from mirroring my pose against her desk to abruptly standing straight and shoving me at the shoulders. "No, you should get going if you don't want to run into Elijah. You know this is the first place he's going to look for you."

And she wasn't wrong. In fact, I was surprised he hadn't come here already. The thought made me smile.

"What are you smiling about?" Rio asked.

"I was thinking of Grant and Elijah busting through that door the way they did the first day I met Elijah." Then I smiled even bigger. "Right here." I tapped on her desk several times. *Tap tap tap.* "In this very kitchen."

"Oh, that's right, ladies and gentlemen," Rio said with a phony mystified tone. She gave me a sideways glance to make sure I was witnessing her playacting. She threw in some jazz hands to really ham it up.

"Sexy and enigmatic Elijah Banks ensnared by this sultry seductress, Hannah Farsey."

I took a turn at the shoulder pushing now, and I nearly knocked the skinny woman off her feet for the second time, which only made me laugh harder. "You are ridiculous. But in all seriousness, you're also right. I need to get out of here. But don't think we won't be talking about this next time we have a few minutes to ourselves. Please, if that bossy green-eyed sex god comes by—"

I couldn't finish what I was saying because Rio's eyes were bugging out so far from what just slipped out of my mouth, I couldn't stop laughing.

She was in stitches too. After wiping the tears from her eyes, she finally said, "What did you just call him? So it's true, isn't it? It's true what the guys call him? You lucky little bitch…" She trailed off, shaking her head from side to side.

"Oh, bullshit! You can't be serious right now. Tell me with a man that tall, he doesn't have an enormous dick? You just be quiet with that whining," I teased.

"All right, all right. You got me. I just had to tease you a little. I love that shade of rose your cheeks turn when you're embarrassed. Although now, I'm not sure if it's embarrassment or if you're getting all hot and horny." Rio waggled her eyebrows while talking.

"Oh my God, do you hear yourself? I'm leaving," I managed to string together between fits of laughter. "Is it okay if I just bring your car back to work with me in the morning? Or I can swing by your place and pick you up?"

"Yes, that will be perfect. Thank you. Then I won't have to get in late because of waiting for the Tree and his two-hour morning self-care ritual."

When I bugged my eyes out in disbelief, she clutched my forearm with a surprisingly strong grip, then crossed over with the other hand too. "I'm telling you, Han, this man has a product graveyard most women would trample each other for."

I had finally settled down from the giggles, but when I saw the gravity in my friend's expression ... I was gone. We both burst out all over again in a fresh wave of raucous laughter.

Rio sobered once more. "Please call me if you need someone to talk to. It doesn't matter what time, okay?"

"I will. I promise," I said with my hand raised in oath as my boss ushered me to the door.

I looked back over my shoulder when I was about halfway across the parking lot and called to her, "Bye! Thanks again!"

Rio waved and ducked back inside.

I'd forgotten this little car was a manual transmission. I stared at the gear shift in between the two front seats like it was a trilobite fossil. "Kendall, are you serious right now? And ... perfect. I'm talking out loud to a car. I swear, I'm keeping my shit together. I'm not going to completely break down because of a man. Hell no."

This had to be like riding a bike. I'd known how to do this once upon a time. The car I owned before my BMW 1 series had a manual transmission, so I just needed to stay calm and ease my foot off the clutch and go. Sitting in this parking lot all night wasn't going to clear my head.

My phone rang inside my bag. It was the ringtone I had for Elijah. He had been trying regularly since I left the courthouse this afternoon. In each ring was another stab to my broken heart.

Talking to him would be dangerous to my resolve, and I knew that. That man had a golden tongue for more than one reason. This one being he could talk his way in or out of any situation. I'd watched him do it several times. Watching from the sidelines was awe inspiring. Being the target of his talent, however, not so much.

I found my way through the side streets and onto the freeway heading north. As I'd explained to Rio, driving oftentimes cleared my head. Traffic was light in both directions since it was well past rush hour. I downshifted to pass the slowpoke in front of me and gunned the gas.

"Come on, Kendall, let's see what you got," I shouted over the playlist Rio had preprogrammed into the stereo. This was definitely music I'd never heard before, but it fit my aggressive, dark, angsty mood. Maybe I should introduce my friend to some upbeat pop music? It might help improve her state of mind. Just a thought . . .

I found myself checking my rearview mirror to ensure my security guy was on my tail but then I remembered no one knew where I was. It was both liberating and terrifying at the same time. But I had to be reasonable about this. There had been no threats, phone calls, or unwanted visitors at our house...

What was I saying? It wasn't *our* house. It was *Elijah's* house. Anyway, no unwanted visitors at his house since Shawna was arrested. It was ridiculous that we were still being so paranoid. We both knew it was an excuse we were using to ease my guilt about living with a man I barely knew.

So how did I already have such intense feelings for him? I had had a few long-term boyfriends in college, so I knew a lot about my own feelings and needs. Of course, Elijah had taught me a lot more about my needs, needs I didn't even know I had. Well, that thought had me smiling and squirming a little bit in the driver's seat.

After driving just under an hour, I decided to turn around and head back. I was getting tired, and the usual peace I felt after a trip in the car just wasn't coming. In fact, I felt more agitated than before. More questions than answers flooded my mind, and I really needed to face the music and sit down and talk to this man. I needed to know the part I played in his life. Maybe if he could define that for me, I could do a better job playing the role.

All I knew was seeing him today and the way he still reacted over that woman broke a big piece of my heart off. It had been years since they broke up. Yet his reaction was like it happened last week. And then the bomb dropped that he had a child with this woman. He never once mentioned having a child. Not one time. How did he expect me to react?

That frustrated me beyond words. Everyone always thought they could walk all over me because I was the nice sister. I was the one who bent over backward for everyone. I gave up my time, I burned my energy—hell, I'd even give the shirt off my back if someone said they needed it. I was used to that bullshit from my family, but I never expected it from Elijah. Never.

I vowed to myself to pick up the phone when it rang the next time. The only way this was going to get better was talking it out. Whether I liked it or not.

Rio had warned me that the gas tank was low. Now it was almost empty. Of course I would not return her car with an empty tank of gas, so I pulled into a well-lit gas station and went through the usual motions of filling the car. I scrolled through the notifications on my phone while waiting for the tank to fill.

Missed call. Missed call. Missed call. Text message. Missed call. Voicemail-Elijah Banks. Notification-Snapchat. Notification-Twitter. Email twelve unread messages.

The pump *thunked* off, letting me know Kendall's belly was full, but one text message from Rio was still unread, and that grabbed my attention. I opened that app and read her message.

> *Hey girl just FYI he was here and he's*
> *not looking so good. You might want*
> *to give him a call. Just saying.*

I looked at the timestamp from the message, and it was just about ten minutes after I left the Inglewood kitchen. Good thing I took off when I did. But now what? Did I call? Text? I was so inexperienced with this kind of thing.

Maybe I should call Agatha. But she was ruthless. People underestimated her because she was so small, she looked harmless. But she was the strongest warrior I knew. My sister would tell me to dump him. No man was worth feeling all the negative things I was currently feeling.

But she would change her tune if she knew all the amazing feelings that man could inspire too. My God, just considering the physical pleasure he brought my body alone would grant him a few get-out-of-jail-free cards. There was so much more to this man than what he could do in bed, though. But the reputation he had with the ladies was for a very good reason.

First, I decided to text Rio and let her know I was going to go to my parents' house in Brentwood and thank her again for letting me use her car. She answered right away, and we planned a time for my morning pick-up. I loved the feature in this car that enabled you to do voice to text while you were driving. My BMW was just a little too old to have this technology in it. Hmmm, maybe it was time for a trade-in. What was better than getting a new car?

Just when I thought I would get away with not being put in the hot seat, one last text came in from Rio.

Have you talked to Elijah?

There was no point in evading her question. Plus, I had nothing to hide. She knew the whole situation, and what I didn't tell her, I was sure Grant would.

Not yet. But he's next on the list.

Wow! I rank above the monster!
I feel so special.

OMG would you stop!

Of course she had me laughing, even though I was telling her to knock it off. I loved Rio's sense of humor, and she had the timing of a professional comedian. She knew how to take the tension out of every situation that needed it.

Well, time to get it over with. I hated that it felt like that in my stomach while initiating a conversation with the man I thought I was falling in love with. It really cemented the fact that we needed to talk this out and fix things. The relationship we were building was too good to lose over a misunderstanding. Christ, I hoped it was a misunderstanding.

I found the conversation with Elijah and then sat there and drew a blank. I couldn't think of what to say, or rather, I had so much to say I didn't know where to start.

Maybe an apology. Maybe I should go home to Malibu— damn it, to Elijah's home—and just talk to him face-to-face. But if I saw him, I knew what would happen. He would tilt his head to the side and his hair would flop over too. He would give me that sexy grin he used to get whatever he wanted, and we'd fall into bed. Ten minutes tops.

Did that make me pathetic? That all I could last in his presence without getting physical with him was ten minutes? I wondered if it would always be this way. Would I always have such a strong magnetic pull toward the man? I knew for certain I'd never felt this way about someone before. I'd even had boyfriends who I had to talk myself into being physical with. How sad was that? Not to mention unfair, for both parties involved.

Hi. I owe you an apology for

my behavior today. I hope you can
forgive me for acting immature
and irrational. I understand if
you're still angry and need time.

Then I scrutinized those four sentences for seven minutes. I wanted to be sure they could not be misunderstood, that the tone was even and could not be taken wrong, and that I said what was most important. Although I really wanted to end it with *I love you*, I showed some restraint and left the ball in his court completely. That should speak to his dominant nature—having the illusion of control of the conversation.

I instructed the car to send the message and finally pulled out of the gas station and headed toward Brentwood. I was lucky the clerk working inside the gas station hadn't called the police because I'd been sitting there so long. He'd kept watching me suspiciously, but seriously, he must have seen way more questionable activity in a shift than a woman sitting in her car scrolling through her phone.

Only a few minutes went by, and my phone signaled I had a text message. It was him.

Hi, honey. Where are you?

I activated the car system and told him my location. I was very close to downtown, so I could go to either Malibu or Brentwood. I wasn't closer to one or the other. But something seemed so strange about his message. That man had never called me honey in all the time I'd known him.

Can you meet me at the Edge?

At Sebastian Shark's building?

Yes. The jobsite downtown.

I can, but what are you doing there?

The last time I had been by that address, it was still largely under construction. Fortunately, I didn't have to do lunch deliveries very often, so I didn't get into the financial district very often. Maybe they had made serious progress on the building.

Elijah answered my curiosity with his next text message.

I got called to the jobsite on a security matter. I figured if you were in the area, we could just meet up.

Okay, that made more sense. I took mental notice of my physical state. I was grinning from ear to ear, and the butterflies in my stomach were dipping and diving like they were kites being flown at the beach. I could even feel my pulse hammering in my neck.

Just at the thought of seeing him. Jesus, I had it bad for this guy. And if I were honest, it scared me to death. I was willingly handing over my emotional and mental stability and well-being to another person—to a man—and it was frightening. It wasn't the man himself, but the idea of giving up that kind of control. I'd watched a lot of friends and even my own sisters go through terrible, ugly breakups and nursed them through broken hearts. Those were favors I never wanted to collect a debt on.

I exited the freeway to wind through the city streets into the financial district. At a red light, I quickly put the nearest intersection I could remember the Edge being near into the navigation app on my phone so I wouldn't get lost. Between my head being in the clouds from the excitement and my terrible sense of direction in general, I was bound to get turned around among all the tall buildings.

Usually, if I could see the horizon, I was in good shape. If you could see the ocean, you knew which way was west. Even if you couldn't see the water itself, you could tell by looking at the sky. Something was just different about the sky's cerulean that reflected off the Pacific.

In less than ten minutes, I was at my destination. Kendall was a lot like my car—small and easy to park almost anywhere. The fact that it was long past working hours made it easy to find a spot on the street as well. I knew from doing lunch deliveries for Abstract that it was a nightmare to find parking around here during the day. I locked the car, dropped the keys into my bag, and pulled out my phone to text Elijah to find out where on this massive property he wanted to meet.

I'm here. Where do you want to meet?

Follow the path around the right side of the security trailer. I let them know you were coming so you don't have to go inside. I'll meet you over there. I'm walking up from the other side of the property now.

After reading the instructions a second time, I set off

in that direction. An eerie sense of foreboding ran up and down my body as I followed the path into an open mouth of darkness. I considered getting out my phone and using the light, but I didn't want to attract attention from the security guards. From what Elijah had said in previous conversations, they were very strict about visitors on this jobsite.

It might not do more than make me feel safer, but I dug through my purse and found the pepper spray I kept in there for situations like this. Not that I found myself in situations like this very often, but it gave me peace of mind.

I distracted myself with remembering the day my dad sat his princess posse—as he had taken to calling us—down and distributed a little canister to each one of us. Even my mom got one, and I think she was the most impressed with his gesture. But that was love for you. He could give her the most ordinary item and say it was a gift just because it reminded him of her, and she immediately had stars in her eyes.

A lot like I did when Elijah did something kind for me.

I chuckled to myself, thinking about the consequences my dad would face for referring to us as his princess posse now. The havoc Sheppard would rain down upon him. The poor man wouldn't even know what hit him other than her knee to his balls. He likely wouldn't understand a single word's meaning of her verbal assault, either. My God, did that girl have a mouth on her when she was mad. Bitter, spiteful, and mean. Straight-up mean. That, in a nutshell, was why we all just stayed away from her.

And how sad was that? We all avoided her as if she had an infectious disease just so we wouldn't upset her. And she was my sister. Our sister. I told myself it wouldn't always be this way, that she would either find a man who brought out the better side in her or discovered a deeper connection to something that gave her a brighter perspective on life.

Occupying my racing brain was the best plan at the moment. Even if it was with thoughts of ways to best handle Shep. If I let my mind wander, it would undoubtedly replay every horror movie I had ever watched and what happened to the stupid girl who didn't listen to her gut. Those same movies were probably to blame for the thoughts going through my head in the first place. Not instinct or intuition or whatever.

It was so incredibly dark, though. I couldn't see more than four feet in front of me. The place was a typical jobsite with a lot of uneven ground and plenty of hazards to stumble over, so I stepped carefully to avoid falling. That would be so like me, too. Acting all tough and brazen all day to this man, and then right before I finally confront him face-to-face, trip and fall and skin my knee and he would find me crying like a little girl.

This was getting worrisome, though, because I thought our paths would have crossed by now. I pulled my phone out of my pocket to check if he messaged me again, but he hadn't. I stood there staring at my phone for far too long. I didn't know what I was hoping the thing would do, when a man's voice came from behind me. He startled me, and I almost dropped my phone, but after a little hot potato with the device, I got a good grip on it again and shoved it into the back pocket of my jeans. All while whirling around to see Elijah behind me.

Only . . . it wasn't Elijah. I had no idea who this guy was.

"Hello," he said. "Hannah, right?"

I took a step back and quickly put my hand that was holding the pepper spray behind my back. All I could hope was that he hadn't already seen it.

"Who are you?" I answered the stranger's question

with one of my own. All while trying my best to sound strong and brave. "Who wants to know?" I followed with a second question so I appeared totally in control of the conversation and, by association, the situation. Not sure this guy was buying it, though.

Another voice came from behind me. "No one said she was this pretty."

Shit, the bad situation just got worse. Now I had a man in front of me and one behind me. I could feel my hands shaking and my heartbeat pick up the pace in my chest. It was the onset of a panic attack, and I wasn't exactly in a position to *distract and delay* at the moment. I had to try to calm myself in other ways I didn't normally use if I was going to make it out of this alive. At the very least, not gang raped.

"You don't want to hang around here," I warned. "My boyfriend is meeting me here any moment, and he's very possessive. And dangerous. Leave now and we can keep this between us."

The creepy guy behind me had gotten closer, and when he cackled—I guess that was his version of laughing—his stench just got stronger, and I had to tamp down my gag reflex. The smell was a gross combination of body odor, bad breath, and some sort of alcohol finished off with a spritz of a cologne that had a main undertone of greasy car mechanic.

My entire body gave an involuntary shudder before I fortified my spine and my resolve. If I showed even a sliver of weakness to these two—oh, wait, make that three men—I would be done for.

The third guy came from the shadows while I was giving myself that last pep talk, and I knew there wasn't a snowball's chance in hell I was getting away from this unscathed.

My God, Elijah, if I die, know that I loved you.

I couldn't just do what they wanted without putting up a fight, though. There was no way. I knew what most people thought when they looked at me. Barbie doll, airhead, dumb blonde. Trust me, I'd heard it all. The element of surprise had always been on my side because of those stereotypes and the dumb people who thought them.

Heaving in a breath and digging deep for some confidence, I asked the one who seemed like he was the leader, "What do you want?"

He walked forward until our toes were nearly touching, and I reared back from him. Apparently he used the same cologne as his buddy. Seriously…was it a prerequisite of being a bad guy? You had to smell bad? If that were the case, these were some really bad guys.

"What do we want?" The guy looked around at his buddies, and they all laughed.

I swear it was like watching a bad movie, they were all so over the top. More like caricatures than characters. If the lighting was better, I could confirm my suspicion, but I swore the one man was actually missing a few of his front teeth.

"Yes, that's what I asked. What do you want? Is it money? I can get money, but you have to let me use a phone so I can arrange it. And I suggest you don't touch me. Not one single finger on me. Because no matter who I call, whether it's my boyfriend or my family, they will insist that I'm returned unharmed."

"Shut up, lady. It doesn't matter who insists on what," smelly guy number three said.

"We don't make the rules around here. We just follow them. That's how we get paid. Our boss says go get the girl"—

he shrugged—"we go get the girl. It's that easy. Today, you're the girl." Toothless poked his index finger into my shoulder so hard, it threw my body off-balance. He stared at me after making the comment, and I had to hold back a retch again.

This time it wasn't just his smell that made my stomach turn over. I was mentally digesting the way he was looking at me, like he wanted to have me for dinner. As if he could hear my thoughts, he rudely licked his bottom lip, and I shuddered.

He took a few steps closer, and I really got a whiff of him then.

I closed my eyes and tried to call up the memory of how Elijah smelled instead. Usually he didn't wear cologne, but the soap he used in the shower each morning stuck with him most of the day.

"You sure are pretty," the disgusting man in front of me said as a cloud of rancid carbon dioxide settled over me along with his words.

All I could think of was getting away. And as quickly as possible before one of these three men got some stupid idea. I already had enough things in my daily life that triggered my anxiety and panic disorders. I didn't need to add fearing all of mankind on top of that, too. Regardless of any self-preservation measures I took, I was probably going to have nightmares based on this incident. But still, I would do everything in my power to come out as unharmed as possible.

Since I refused to look at the creepy man's face, especially while he was standing so close to me, I had a long look at the ground where we stood and the dirt between us. On his feet he wore some sort of combat boots or maybe work boots, but definitely not athletic shoes. One was tied as it should be, and the other was open and looked like the lace had broken off at a crucial point, so a repair wasn't possible. There was no way that shoe would be stable for running, and that was the fact that stuck with me. If I could incapacitate one and have one chase me, I'd want this guy to chase me because he wouldn't be very fast in that footwear. As for the third guy? Well, he remained the problem and the wild card.

I came up with a plan and set it into motion before I had a chance to talk myself out of it. Time was of the essence, and it was running out quickly. I didn't have extra minutes to be rational or thoughtful about any of it.

Playing the innocent girl never really worked for me, even though I looked like everyone's kid sister—or at least that was what I'd been told. I had a hard time believing it myself, though. I had my fingers crossed that it worked for me this time, though, because it was a major part of my plan.

I backed away from the smelly, toothless man one cautious step at a time until I bumped into the other guy just like I expected to. Quickly I spun around on the balls of my feet and caught the guy by surprise. He must have thought I was going to freeze in terror when I touched his body, but so far, the scene was playing out exactly how I envisioned it.

So when he reached both arms up to my shoulders to steady me, thinking I was going to topple over, I knew it was now or never to make my move. With his arms parallel to the ground and at shoulder height, his entire body was vulnerable for an attack.

At that point, I grabbed onto his biceps to steady myself and reared back to deliver a solid knee to his crotch with as much force as I possibly could. Then I brought my leg down and did it again. I was ready to do it a third time when he slumped to the ground and rolled off to one side. His face was flame red from the combination of pain and lack of oxygen and possibly a good dose of anger. Hell if I knew, and bigger hell if I was staying around to find out.

If my calculations were correct, that left the third, quiet guy. He hadn't said much so far, but I could almost hear my dad saying something like *It's the quiet ones you have to watch out for*. When I turned back to face them, I saw them conferring, and my heart galloped inside my chest. I didn't think it could beat any harder than it had been, but the damn thing was out to prove me wrong.

They had joined forces and were advancing on me as one, and I hadn't accounted for that possibility. Panic churned in my stomach and bile flowed up into my throat, but I couldn't allow myself to get sick and show weakness. There would be enough time after I got out of this mess for losing my shit.

Originally my plan was going to be to spray the one guy in the face with my pepper spray and just run as fast as I could and get away from the other one whose shoe was untied. There was no way he was going to be able to keep up with me in those shoes. I was sure of it. But now with them both here, basically in range of one stream of pepper spray, I would be able to hit them both at the same time repeatedly, which would give me even more advantage to getting away.

If one needed more than the other, it would have to be the guy with the good shoes. He would have to be the one to go down with the larger dose of pepper spray. And then I had to book it out of there as fast as I could. The next biggest challenge would be finding my way off this jobsite, which seemed to be getting darker the longer we were out here.

I fiddled with the canister in my pocket and got the small cylinder in my grip and ready to spray. I knew this thing had a range of about fifteen feet, so I didn't have to let these slimeballs get too close to me before I could hurt them. I just needed both to go down to the ground and be blinded so I could run away. If it was reasonable, I would hit their buddy, who was still on the ground crying about his balls, on my way out.

"Easy, girl, no more funny business. You just cooperate with us, and we won't hurt you. But if you pull another stunt like that"—Toothless looked back at his friend on the ground and then back to me to finish his threat—"things are going to get a lot harder for you."

"Yeah," the third guy contributed to the conversation. Well shit, maybe he wasn't as smart as I was trying to make him out to be.

"Oh, fuck off!" I spat back, wanting to keep them engaged in the conversation and antagonize them enough so they would come closer to me. Well, it worked, because they both took a ground-eating, menacing step toward me.

"Dude, get the fuck up. We need to get out of here, and we are not carrying your sorry ass. Stop being a pussy."

"I'm not being a pussy. I think she broke something. I've been kicked in the balls a few times in my life, and it's never hurt like this."

I had to admit I was a little proud of myself hearing that. I must have gotten him good. My old self-defense instructor would be so proud. But it was time to put that pepper-spray training into good use too. I tried to be stealthy with my movement, but the quiet one noticed right away when I was putting my hand in my pocket and smacked Toothless with t he backs of his fingers.

"I said no funny business, girl. Put your hands where I

can see them. Now," the toothless wonder instructed. Of course, I had no intention of complying. The next time he saw my hand, I would be introducing the mucous membranes of his face to my old friend pepper spray.

"We could tie her up. Or let's just get out of here. Let's get to the car and take off."

"No," I whimpered. "Please, I'll do anything. Just let me go. I won't tell anyone that I saw you—I won't tell them your descriptions. I promise. You'll go free. No one will know it was you. Just let me go. Let me go now."

Most of that untrue promise rushed out in one long sentence. I was doing my best to not panic or let my anxiety run away with me, but it wasn't easy. I kept telling myself repeatedly I could get through this. I could get through this.

I can get through this.

"I'm afraid not, sweetheart," the quiet guy lamented. "When we're hired to do a job, we finish the job. Now, do we need to gag you so you don't make a scene when we leave this place?"

"I'm not leaving here with you," I said defiantly and punctuated the statement with a stiff lower jaw and set shoulders.

That must have been the last straw for Toothless. When he started toward me, so did his buddy. I aimed the pepper spray canister, flipped up the little plastic trigger guard, and sprayed the quiet guy first and then the toothless guy. I repeated the action over and over until they fell to the ground yelling and whimpering about their burning faces.

While they were preoccupied with their own discomfort, I quickly pulled out my cell phone, brought up the phone feature, and snapped a few pictures of them focusing mainly on their faces. If I got out of this situation intact—no, *when* I got out of this situation intact—I would be able to show the authorities who did this. Served them right as far as I was concerned. What kind of kidnapper allowed their captive to keep their own cell phone? Even I knew that was a big, dumb mistake.

Their buddy, the crotch king, was on his feet and cautiously coming toward me, walking with his legs bent together to touch at the knees, and it was the funniest thing I'd ever seen.

I wished I had time to stop and laugh at him properly, but I couldn't take my chances. Instead, I quickly took his picture too and then sprayed him in the face with my pepper spray.

Poor guy couldn't tell which end was up at that point.

Then I took off running.

"You little bitch!" one of them yelled.

It didn't matter which one was yelling as long as they weren't in close pursuit while doing it. I had no idea which way to turn when I came to an open area within the steel framework of the building. It had been months since I'd seen the architect's rendition of what the whole place would look like when it was done, so I couldn't picture where I might be . . . and therefore where a street might be.

I felt like I was caught in a carnival's house of mirrors. For one thing, it was very dark. This jobsite used to be like a beehive in a spotlight at every hour of the day. But Elijah said after a woman took her life here and Rio's husband was killed here too, things scaled back from the hurry-up-and-get-it-done mind-set.

When grave mistakes were made, everyone stepped back and asked themselves what they could do to make the site a safer place. They also asked themselves what was more important—adding another rooftop to the downtown skyline or making sure everyone stayed alive?

A sharp skid, and I turned right and hustled deeper into the darkness. I decided to risk being trapped in a dead end when I saw a stairwell up ahead. It became obvious this would be a corner of the building where the emergency staircase was typically built. I looked up into the night sky, and the flight went as far as I could see. Even rocking back on my heels, I couldn't see the top.

That was okay, though. I was interested in the bottom. The very bottom that was right here in front of me. A slow smile spread across my lips, and it might have been the first one all day.

I recalled the house I grew up in before my family moved to Brentwood. There was a closet under the staircase, and Agatha and I loved playing in there because we thought we were hiding from our mom. Of course, later we found out she knew where we were the entire time. When our mom first dropped that little truth bomb, she totally spoiled years of memories for my sister and me.

Now that years had passed and we were both older, we were able to understand the special gift our mom gave us. Quiet time with each other undisturbed by the other girls, in a safe place, still under her watchful eye, all while giving us a sense of independence and maturity. I didn't know how she'd learned the fine art of motherhood, but I was so glad I had her to help me when that time came in my life. I didn't feel like it was a natural thing a woman possessed just because she was female. Some women seemed better at it than others—or at least better suited for it.

If I didn't get myself out of this situation in one piece,

motherhood wouldn't be a blip on my radar. Because I would no longer be on anyone's radar either. One sweep here, the next sweep—gone.

But I had to cut that crap right here. There would be plenty of time to get morose later. Right now, I had to hide. I eyed the space beneath the stairs from where I stood and considered just how tiny it was. Shaking off my nerves, I decided it was still my best option. Claustrophobia had never been on my list of issues, and hell if that list wasn't getting longer by the hour lately. But still . . . the area was so small.

I decided to crawl in backward so I could still see out once I was settled into position. If I went in headfirst, there was no way I'd be able to turn around in that cramped spot. Then I'd be staring at a concrete wall until I thought it was safe to come out. Every little bump and bang out on the jobsite would make me a nervous wreck. I would convince myself those creeps had finally found me and had come back to finish the job.

First, I made sure I had my cell phone, and thankfully it was still in my back pocket. The way things were going today, it wouldn't have surprised me if it had jostled out when I sprinted across the jobsite. So, trying to plan ahead, I set the phone on the ground near the stairs and got down on the ground to shimmy beneath the lowest one.

Already, I planned on distracting myself with fantasies of luxuriating in a big, hot jacuzzi bathtub. If he was extra remorseful when I spoke to him, I'd let Elijah share it with me.

Even though it was late August, the concrete floor was surprisingly cool. Since this staircase was at the corner of the building, it was shielded from the evening breeze that could always be felt in Los Angeles being so close to the ocean.

With trepidation, I woke my phone to see how much

power I had left and if I had service. As expected, I had about twenty percent of my battery's strength left. Pretty typical for a long day like this one had been. But I needed to be mindful and only use the phone for emergencies. I wouldn't be checking my Instagram or Twitter.

That ridiculous thought made me chuckle out loud, and I quickly put my hand over my mouth. The last thing I needed was to give myself away by laughing at my own dumb joke. I scrolled through my recent call list and found Elijah's name. I had one bar of signal strength, so I pressed call and hoped for the best. If I couldn't get a call out, I was so screwed.

After two rings, the call dropped. I pulled the device away from my ear to look to be sure that was what happened. So that went the routine three more times before I gave up on his number and tried my parents' house. Again, the phone rang twice and I lost the connection.

Even though I was getting very frustrated, I didn't have another option, so I took a calming breath and tried again. By some stroke of luck, on the third ring, Sheppard answered the phone.

"Yeah?"

"Sheppard! Thank God you answered," I rushed out before she could hang up on me. Heaven knew it wouldn't be the first time. "Oh, thank God." Fighting back tears, I asked, "Are Mom or Dad there?"

"Do I look like their personal assistant, Han-nah?" She always said my name in two choppy syllables like it was extra effort to get them both out.

Keeping my tone very serious, I said, "Look, now is not the time for this. I need help. I'm in a bad situation, and I need help."

"Oh, boo-hoo. What else is new with you? Did that boyfriend of yours tell you he saw me tonight?"

"What? No, he didn't. I—" But 1 didn't get to finish what I was saying because she bulldozed right over me with her next comment.

"Oooh, why am I not surprised? He's a player, Han-nah. I mean, look at him. He's prettier than most girls. I saw him at dinner with another woman. A stunning woman, I might add. Let him try to deny it." I could feel her gloating across the phone line.

"Sheppard. Please. I don't have time for this right now. I need to speak to Dad or Mom. I'm not joking. This is an emergency." I was becoming frantic at that point.

She sighed so heavily I almost thought I could feel the moisture from her breath on my ear. "Uugghh, Hannah. When is it not with you? Why don't you call that cheating boyfriend of yours? I gotta go."

And then she hung up. She fucking hung up on me! The one call I could get to connect, and she hung up on me. That little bitch. She was going to regret this, and when my parents found out what had happened, she'd be lucky if they didn't kick her out of their house. She had a serious problem, but that was on her. That was something she was going to have to work through. Right now, I had to deal with the problem I was smack dab in the middle of.

He went out to dinner with her.

If there was anything in my stomach, I would have thrown it up. And that wasn't the biggest of my worries either. I needed to outlast these creeps and get away from Sebastian Shark's Edge and whatever all of this had to do with the man.

Including his best friend.

CHAPTER NINE

ELIJAH

By the time we called it a night up on the roof of Shark Enterprises, it was after midnight. I figured if Hannah had gone back to the house in Malibu, I would find a warm, luscious body in my bed. If she'd decided to be immature about the whole situation at the courthouse today and stomp back to her parents' house in a huff, then I would deal with her in the morning. At least I would be completely sober and probably better equipped mentally and emotionally to handle a conversation with her.

Memories of my father snaked up my spine, and I gave a physical shudder in the back seat of my blacked-out SUV. Marc had come downtown to give me a lift since I'd been drinking.

I hadn't gained much insight by telling Grant and Bas the whole situation from the afternoon. The benefit I had received, however, was the support of my two lifelong best friends. And that was priceless.

Going into it, I hadn't really expected answers from them necessarily. Typically when we all got together and talked out a particularly troubling concern, we all found that just talking about it to each other helped iron out the wrinkles. I couldn't say this problem was a crisp linen sheet now, but it was better than the shirt at the bottom of the dirty laundry basket that it was right after I'd had dinner with my ex.

When I got home, first up on the agenda would be a hot shower and then some protein to soak up the alcohol I'd just carelessly abused my body with. After a good night's sleep, I'd start tomorrow morning off with some good old-fashioned groveling. It had never been my strongest talent, but for Hannah, I'd give the tried-and-true parlor trick a spin around the track. I certainly knew how to be charming. Maybe if I approached it as a version of that honed skill, I could excel at it.

Checking my voicemail for the third time, I found it was still empty. But in the call log, I saw three missed calls from Hannah—all back to back.

Why didn't she leave a message?

The missed-call log entry showed the duration of each call to be zero or one second. Almost like the call didn't have a chance to connect before she hung up. Hannah wasn't the kind of woman to play games like we were in high school. She wouldn't call my voicemail and then hang up.

Something was odd about those calls. The fact that they came in one after the other added to the confusion—9:07 p.m., 9:07 p.m., and 9:08 p.m. We were on the roof by then, I had my phone with me, and the ringer was on. Bas and Grant had both received calls while we were up there, so I knew there was nothing wrong with the service.

Well, no Hannah waiting for me in bed. Bummer for me. Big bummer. My head was starting to throb, so I decided to try to figure out this phone call situation in the morning. Hell, I would just talk to the woman directly then and not play CSI.

Marc got me home in good time, and I was out the minute my head hit the pillow.

My cell phone's incessant ringing woke me within what

felt like five minutes after I went to sleep.

"Jesus fuck. Turn it off. Hannah, your phone is ringing..."
I mumbled into the pillow, but the damn phone just kept
ringing. I groped for my woman's sleeping body beside me to
wake her, but the bed was empty.

Shiiiit. How had I forgotten? She hadn't slept here last
night. Maybe that was her calling. But why in the middle of the
night? I squinted my eyes to see the clock on the nightstand.
"Six thirty a.m.? Are you kidding? Six thirty," I said—no,
groaned—to no one in particular because again, my woman
hadn't come home last night.

Where was the logic in that? She was mad at me, so she
stayed out all night. That seemed ass-backwards to me. But
then again, who was I? Other than a really rich guy with a
really bad hangover ... and no girlfriend.

Jesus Christ, was that Scotch last night or Mad Dog? I
hoped those two motherfuckers felt as shitty as I did right now.
I finally found my phone buried in the covers and squinted to
see the display.

Jacob Cole?

Why the hell would Jacob Cole be calling me this early in
the morning? I mashed the redial key when I could focus on
the thing long enough and held the phone to my ear.

"Good morning. Jacob Cole," the friendly guy chirped
from the other end of the line.

I had to admit there were times, this being one of them, I
wanted to stab this guy in the eye. He was good-looking, well
dressed, smart as hell, and nicer than any one person needed
to be. All the time. And the real rub? It was genuine. This dude
was really that nice. Not an ounce of bullshit in his routine. I
didn't know if he was taking medication or smoked a ton of

weed every morning—it just wasn't normal. But maybe we all needed to get on board his program. The world would be a much nicer place.

I rubbed my forehead and yawned. "Hey, Cole. Morning, man. It's Elijah Banks. Looks like you just called? Not sure if that was intentional?"

"Yeah, hey, sorry about that. I know it's early, but I thought this was definitely the exception, not the rule. I—well, I—this is awkward," he stammered, and if he were within my reach, I'd shake him. I could still be sleeping instead of listening to this.

"Spit it out, man. It's all good. I need to get up and get into the office anyway. And as luck would have it, I forgot to set my alarm last night, so you totally saved my ass."

"Oh, good, good. Okay, so the reason I'm calling, I was doing a walk-through over at the Edge this morning. I wanted to see a few things before my meeting with Mr. Shark first thing, you know, just to be extra prepared with a few details?"

"Jake, dude. You're killing me . . ."

"Sorry. Anyway. I found a woman hiding in one of the stairwells, and she asked me to call you. She said her name is Hannah? Do you know—"

"You found her where? Is she there right now? Right there with you now? Can you put her on the phone? Is she okay? Can she talk to me?" I fired so many questions at the guy he didn't answer any of them.

"Yeah, yeah. Here you go." Before Hannah began talking to me, I could faintly hear Jake speaking to her in the background. The words were impossible to make out, but his tone was so gentle and considerate. Something about his mannerism with her felt like I was being stabbed straight through my heart with a wooden stake.

"Han? You there?" I finally said when the line continued to stay quiet.

"H-H-Hi," she whispered.

From that one word—no, screw that, from the way she was currently existing in the atmosphere we shared, I knew something was wrong. Very wrong.

"Beautiful, what's going on? What's happened?" I was already in my walk-in closet pulling a pair of jeans out of my dresser and, just as quickly, a fitted white T-shirt from the perfectly folded stack on the back shelf.

"I'm okay. I'm fine. But do you think you could call Dah or my mom or dad? I need a ride, and my phone isn't working."

The growl that came up from deep inside had its own intention as I began to speak. "Is there a reason I can't come get you?"

"Well, I thought you didn't . . ."

"Stop. Just stop. Where are you, baby?"

"Uhhh—"

"I'm getting in the car already. Please give Jacob his phone back and hang tight. I'll be there soon. Okay?" I waited for a reply and then repeated myself, "Hannah? Okay?"

"Fine, yes, okay." She sighed, completely defeated. I couldn't tell if it was the situation or my existence that was snuffing her spirit out, though.

"Mr. Banks? Hey, it's Jake."

"Call me Elijah, man. Shit, call me whatever you want at this point. It sounds like you saved my woman's life by finding her. I'm on my way from Malibu, so it may be a little bit. Thirty minutes maybe?"

"All right. Yeah, no problem." The young architect lowered his voice, and I had to stop shuffling around and listen. "If you don't mind, I would rather take her back to my place and wait for you there." He exhaled heavily. "It doesn't look like she's been assaulted, but she has been outside all night and seems like she has some emotional or psychological bumps and bruises from whatever happened."

I cut him off right there. I couldn't stand hearing another man talk about my girlfriend as if he knew her. It didn't matter if he was spot-on or not or if he had her best interest at heart. I was back to wanting to rip his throat out and floss with his jugular vein.

Fortunately, I pulled my head out of my jealous ass and gave an appropriate response instead. "Yeah, good idea. Do whatever you think is best, man. Can you first text me your address so I can drive there? I really can't thank you enough. I don't know how I'll repay you for this, but I swear, I will."

"Don't be ridiculous. If I had a woman I cared about the way you obviously care about this one, I'd want someone to do the same for me. We have to help each other out, don't we?"

What's this *we* crap? He sounded like a waitress at TGI Fridays. *Are we ready to order?* I pictured a teenage girl, complete with a bad perm and order pad, standing at the end of our table. I could feel my pulse throbbing in the vein in my temple. This level of stress was going to end me early.

"Hello?" Cole said, obviously thinking he'd dropped our call.

"Sorry, man. You're right. In a perfect world, that's what we'd do," I agreed. "I'll be there as soon as I can." And then I did disconnect the call.

But Jacob Cole had no idea who he was talking to. I hated being indebted to anyone. Almost as much as I despised needing help in the first place. I took care of me. No one else did. That lesson was thrust upon me at a very young age. After that, I knew that depending on other people just led to disappointment. Really, the only person you could count on was yourself.

There probably wasn't a traffic law that I didn't break on my way to the address Jacob had sent me. I was guessing it was his apartment or an extended-stay hotel. I couldn't really tell by the outside of the building—it looked like it could have gone either way. Just last night, Sebastian said he thought the guy was still camped out in a hotel. Shit. Was that less than twelve hours ago?

Regardless, I knocked on the door and shifted my weight from one foot to the other and then back again while I waited the eighteen seconds it took for him to answer the door.

Yes, I counted.

My nerves were like a live wire. Not knowing what kind of situation I was walking into felt a little bit like Russian roulette. Especially with a woman like Hannah. I'd seen her have some epic meltdowns, and I didn't relish another.

Cautiously, the door was opened until the secondary lock stopped its progress. I saw Hannah on the other side and completely forgot how to breathe. It looked like she wasn't doing much better than me.

"Elijah. What are you doing here?" There was actually hostility in her voice, and it surprised and angered me at the same time.

"Are you going to let me in, or are you going to make me stand out in the hall? I came for you because you asked me to. Not to mention, how can you even ask me that?" I felt the way my mouth was hanging open in disbelieving shock, and I couldn't correct the posture I was so confused.

"Oh, right," she said as if waking from a stupor. "I'm sorry he called you. I didn't tell him to do that. I know you're very busy since your girlfriend is back."

My frustration swelled like a countryside creek after a summertime downpour. Yeah, there was definitely going to be a flash flood if she kept up this bullshit.

"Hannah…" I warned in the darkest, lowest register possible. And I felt like the biggest ass the moment I saw her reaction.

It took me years of therapy to work through the difference between what anger and frustration felt like when you were sitting in the middle of each emotion. While they were definitely brothers, they weren't twins. So while I had that worked out for myself, I didn't always hit the mark when it came to differentiating the two when it came to my body language, facial expressions and, most importantly, my words.

I assumed her response was because I missed the target and my reaction looked and sounded like anger. Because I already knew anger didn't belong here, and I could fix what I could identify.

Frustration, however, had tickets for seats in the front row. After the shit show of a breakup I went through with Hensley, I swore I would never again cancel my emotions because they were uncomfortable for someone else to experience alongside me. I swore to always live honestly. Like it or not, there were times that meant dealing with unpleasant feelings.

Well, welcome to the big bad world, Ms. Farsey. Strap in, darling. There's rough terrain ahead.

"Open the door. Now."

"Listen, I've had a really long night, and I just want to call my parents so someone can come pick me up," Hannah said in the quietest voice I'd ever heard from her.

"Last warning or I will break it down. You'll want to stand back."

"For God's sake," she huffed while opening the door and gesturing for me to come in.

"Where's Jake?" I asked, looking around the room.

The place was definitely a hotel room with a kitchenette. These places were peppered throughout the city for long-term business travel and, honestly, were an ingenious concept to accommodate the extended stays some jobs required.

"You just missed him. He said he was running behind schedule for a meeting with Shark and looked like he was going to piss himself about it."

She chuckled a fraction, and the sound came out strangled and painful. Painful to me at least, but I didn't have a chance to wallow in the stabbing hurt for long when she jabbed me with the next one.

"What can I do for you, Elijah? Why are you here?" she asked and stared directly into my eyes while doing so. No nervous fidgeting, no pacing back and forth, no stammering or stumbling over her words. This was full-on confrontation.

All right, Farsey. Let's do this.

In two strides, I was toe-to-toe with her. Immediately, she took a step back, and I advanced into the empty space. We repeated this dance until her back was against the wall and she had nowhere else to go.

You'd think by now she would have learned to not get into this position with me. I was mindful about the information Jake had given me and didn't crowd her like I would have in the past. But that didn't mean I couldn't use words.

"Look at me, girl."

I didn't know if she was just being defiant or she truly didn't want to look at me, but she kept her eyes trained on my kneecaps.

That's okay, beautiful. I've got nothing but time.

"No, fuck this," I growled, and that brought her eyes up to mine with a snap of her neck that I heard.

The blue eyes that could be so playful and cool like the Pacific Ocean just a few miles west of here currently looked more like the most intense part of a flame. That place that burned so hot it could forge steel or separate natural elements from the ore where they were found.

My index finger hooked under her chin to ensure her gaze stayed right on me, and I insisted again, "Tell me what's going on. Either tell me what happened last night, tell me why you left the courthouse without me, tell me where you've been since I saw you getting into a cab... Fuck, beauty, tell me something." Well, I started out strong, at least. By the end of the rant, I sounded like a begging pussy.

It wasn't until that moment when I really saw the emotion spark back to life in her whole face. To be honest, I considered taking a step back from her because she looked absolutely homicidal. Paired with the way she began to tremble, and I was really concerned. I offered my strong arms to embrace her, and she immediately batted them away.

"Don't fucking touch me! Don't touch me!" she screeched in a voice I'd never heard from her before, and one much louder than necessary.

Banshee, is that you?

"Hannah. Beautiful. Tell me what's going on. Tell me how to help you right now."

"I did tell you. But you didn't listen, did you? No! You

had to get your bossy way and get inside this room…exactly where I didn't want you. Are you happy? Are you happy now? Now that you got your way…like you're so used to always getting?"

Her chest was heaving in and out with every breath she took. Rosy cheeks, flared nostrils—the girl looked like a raging bull. Seriously, if I weren't so concerned about her mental health and stability at this exact moment, I'd be wildly turned on by her physical appearance.

I'd loved the angry fuck sessions Hensley and I used to have. The pheromones a woman's body sent out when she was this angry spoke to me louder than any other time. What could I say? I was a sexual deviant, and I knew it. Most of the time, I embraced it. As did the women I exposed that side of my personality to.

Hannah didn't even know that part of me existed. I prayed to God she didn't keep up this angry kitty bit she had going on, though. Especially since we were the only two people here, and I knew on some level she'd had a really trying night.

"Okay, let's calm down. Do you want to sit down? Can I get you something? Some water? How about a cup of tea?" I walked over to where the single-serve coffeepot was set up and wrinkled my nose while looking at the selection of pods.

"I don't need you to wait on me, Elijah," she said with attitude. "I'm fine."

"No offense, my love, but you don't look fine. Why did Jacob tell me he found you in a stairwell at the Edge? Did I misunderstand him?" There were bottles of water in the minifridge, and I grabbed two and sat down on the sofa. Out of habit, Hannah sat down with me, and I handed her one of the open bottles.

"Thank you," she said so quietly I almost didn't hear her.

"Wouldn't you rather just go home? I mean to Malibu. I'll run a nice bath for you, wash your hair, give you the works." I wiggled my fingers in the air between us in an attempt to be playful, but she didn't even lift a corner of her mouth to try to smile.

"Then I'll tuck you into bed so you can get some rest. Please, beautiful, let me care for you."

There was some sort of battle going on in her mind. I was getting glimpses of it by way of the expressions that were escaping in between times when she remembered to be stoic. Then I was treated to an acidic comment.

"I'm not your problem anymore. You made that very clear."

"I'm so damn confused. Can you please tell me what you're talking about? You have never been my *problem*. You've been my *joy*. You're the reason I've been happy, truly happy, for the first time in years."

"All I did was ask you to call my sister or my parents to come get me. I didn't need you to come here yourself. I don't need your charity services anymore, Mr. Banks. Go be with the woman you've been searching for for years."

Hannah pressed her index finger to her chin as if really deep in thought and then said abruptly, "I believe that was the way you expressed that?" She tilted her head to the side and looked at me in direct challenge.

"Oh, here we go," I argued back. "That's what this is all about?"

How did I not connect these dots sooner? I couldn't say I blamed her. It was a really shitty thing to say to your current girlfriend. At the same time, she never let me explain myself.

She just ran off, and that wasn't fair by any stretch of the imagination.

Hannah set her water down and stood. She thrust her hands to her hips and fired, "What is that supposed to mean?" Adrenaline must have given her a good shot of energy, because she was plenty spry now.

"It means finally I have something to go on. Are you going to let me explain, or are you going to continue to unfairly judge me?"

"What's to explain? Seems pretty simple, doesn't it? And don't you dare say that's not what you meant or that's not what you said, because I heard you. Loud and clear. I was standing right there while you were having your manic episode or whatever that was . . . just from the sight of the woman!"

She thought for a moment and then looked at me with an expression I truly had never seen on her face before. Frankly, it frightened me. I knew whatever she was about to say was going to leave permanent damage.

"That's the woman you've talked about before. The one who lied to you? Yet she still has that effect on you? I can't help but wonder who the real liar is here, because you're definitely not being honest with yourself." She walked over to the door, opened it, and stood there, but I just stared at her.

"You may go now," she said matter-of-factly. "I can take care of myself."

"No, goddammit. Tell me what happened last night. Why did Jacob find you in that stairwell?"

"Like I said before, I'm not your burden anymore. Go be with your family. Obviously it's where your heart is."

"At least let me drive you home," I implored, thinking if I could have a little more time to explain what happened, she would see how wrong she was. "To your parents' house, I mean, if you don't want to stay in Malibu." I was hopeful since she didn't shoot the idea down right away.

"Where's your purse? Do you have a bag?" I scanned the small space but didn't see anything I recognized as hers. When I looked back at Hannah and really took in what she was wearing, I realized that wasn't her clothing either. Last time I'd seen her, she had on a beautiful gray dress. Now she was wearing men's gym shorts and a T-shirt that was big enough for three of her sisters to wear with her.

"Whose clothing are you wearing?" The question came out sounding like a growly accusation, but it was justified this time. Seeing my woman—yes, mine—in another man's clothing tripped a trigger I didn't know I possessed.

My beauty looked down as though she couldn't remember what she had on and jolted. What an odd reaction. If I found out that Jacob Cole had helped himself to her body while she was unconscious or something remotely seedy, I'd kill him. It was always the innocent-looking ones you had to keep your eye on. I'd learned that lesson early on.

"Knock it off," Hannah scolded and backhanded my abdomen then pushed past me to recycle our water bottles in the kitchenette.

"Knock what off?" I rubbed my stomach.

"You were growling. Over what, I have no idea. Nor do you have any possession over me, so . . . yeah, definitely stop." She opened the door and walked out. From down the exterior passageway, I heard her call back, "Are you coming?"

Not nearly soon enough.

By the time I shifted into gear and swept my gaze around the room one last time for anything forgotten, I stepped out into the corridor, and she was gone. I hustled to the end and just caught sight of her stepping onto the elevator.

"Hold the elevator, please," I called, and there was no way she didn't hear me. But just as I came into view, the doors were sliding shut and she was staring right at me. She didn't make a single effort to stop the car from departing.

While I waited for the damn thing to return from the lobby, I came up with at least three creative ways to redden her ass for this bratty routine she had going on today. I had a good sense something terrible had happened last night, though, and I knew I had to use a big dose of patience with her until I found out the whole story. I didn't know how else to get her to talk to me, though. I couldn't figure out why she was holding back the details, especially if she had been in danger. She knew how serious I was about her safety.

But that raised another question . . .

Once we were settled in my car and had pulled onto the street, I gave her a few pointed glances. She, on the other hand, was completely fascinated with the scenery passing by on her side of the street.

I reached over and touched her thigh. "Han?"

She skittered back from my touch like I was a comic book villain and had fire for fingertips. "Don't touch me!" she shouted and then flopped back in her seat and cradled her face in her hands.

At the first safe place, I pulled off to the side of the road, rammed the car into park, and turned to face her completely.

"Look at me, please," I said quietly.

Her crying sniffles were steady but not so loud that she didn't hear me.

"Hannah. I said look at me. Stop being so defiant. I'm

trying to help you."

I waited for a few moments until I felt like I'd explode from the potent mixture of this male protectiveness, the strong desire to correct her defiant attitude and, most of all, the all-consuming love I felt for this woman.

This was not the time to lay that sentiment on her, but I was getting desperate enough to throw it down. I'd keep it as my ace in the hole and bring it out as a last resort. I'd been on the couch enough hours to know words were not weapons or tools of manipulation, so every good guy part of me was screaming *don't do it, man.*

"Did someone hurt you last night? Will you at least tell me that? And why wasn't Marc with you?" Damn it, I should've stuck with one question at a time. Now I'd probably overwhelmed her again or given her a good enough reason to answer one and skip the other two when they were all important.

"I never saw any of your men after I got in the cab at the courthouse. I managed to be on my own without a babysitter all day. Would you look at that?"

"I have to assume this nasty attitude is how you're choosing to act out because of my breakdown yesterday in front of the courthouse. I understand why that upset you." I took a calming breath in through my nose and let it out through my mouth. Repeated the same process again before speaking. "I would like a chance to explain what was going on in here"—I thumped my chest with my open hand—"when I said the things that I said. Can you either let me explain that or tell me how you ended up in that stairwell overnight?" I mean, something had to give here. There were too many unanswered questions and loose ends.

Unfortunately, she folded her arms across her chest and continued giving me the silent treatment. I couldn't be the only one who wanted to fix this. We both had to want it.

"Where's your car?" How this was the first time I thought of that question, I had no idea. I could have walked by it twice this morning and never noticed. God knew last night was a bust with the way I felt this morning. I must have had way more to drink than I'd realized.

"What do you mean? Isn't it still at the house?" she asked in alarm.

I squeezed the bridge of my nose before admitting, "I don't really know. I had way too much to drink last night. I wasn't my sharpest when I left the house this morning after Jake called."

"Where were you last night?" she asked, and I didn't miss the tone of accusation in her words.

I stared at her in disbelief. She had to be kidding. She was going to interrogate me when I couldn't even get a straight answer as to her safety? I shook my head slowly from left to right in case she missed the look on my face.

She sighed heavily and looked out the window as she mumbled, "This is ridiculous."

"This *is* ridiculous. This whole fucking thing is ridiculous because you won't listen to me. You won't give me the benefit of the doubt and let me explain myself to you." In frustration, I banged my closed fist on the steering wheel. I must have hit the circumference in the perfect spot, because the reverberation made the horn sound even though I wasn't pressing the center.

"You are being unfair." *Pound. Beep.* "And immature." *Pound. Beep.* "You know how seriously I take your safety." *Pound. Beep.*

"Stop it!" Hannah cried out. "You're scaring me."

I leaned forward and rested my forehead on the steering wheel. How did we get here? How did we get to this place? It was as though we were fighting over how much I cared about her. But no matter what I said, she wouldn't listen to me. I didn't do anything wrong, and she wouldn't let me prove that to her.

I could feel the emotion building up at the base of my throat, and it was seconds away from strangling me completely. I loved this woman. I was convinced she was it for me, and I would not let Hensley fucking Pritchett take her away from me. I had already given up too much of my life to that woman. I'd be damned if I would let her take Hannah away from me too.

CHAPTER TEN

HANNAH

I was scared to death and didn't know who I could trust. Add heartbroken to the mix, and you really got a big confusing mess. That was exactly where I was sitting at the moment. Elijah yelling and banging on things wasn't helping matters, either.

How could I open up to him? How could I trust him? He was the one who'd sent me the message to go to that jobsite last night. He was the one who'd lured me into that danger. I didn't know what kind of sick game he was playing right now, but I didn't want to be a part of it anymore. I just needed to get to my car or get to my parents' house and get far away from him.

The part of my heart that he still owned, and trust me, it was an enormous part, wanted to hear him out. We were so good together, and it was killing me to come to terms with our relationship being over. I'd let myself believe he was the one for me. I'd let myself fall in love with him.

Well, the joke was on me, wasn't it? I should have known better. Before I'd met him, I'd made peace with the fact that I would never have a man in my life. My past left too much damage, too many scars for me to have a normal relationship with a man. I'd tried before; I knew how it would end. Elijah had seemed different, though. And maybe he was. But in the end, I was still the same broken girl as before.

"Beauty, please. Please, listen to me. There is nothing left in my heart for anyone but you. Just you. Seeing Hensley freaked me out. And I will admit I lost my shit there for a while. But not because she ignited some old flame just by seeing her. Quite the opposite." He chuckled.

He was actually laughing.

"I'm glad you're amused by all of this, Elijah."

"Please stop. Please stop looking for a fight. I was chuckling at the notion of me still caring about that woman. I despise her. No, more than that. There isn't a word that accurately quantifies how much I loathe her. If you don't believe me—which I can't understand why you wouldn't, when I have preached to you how I feel about dishonesty—talk to Grant or Bas. They'll tell you without any lead-in how much I hate that woman."

"Is that how your relationships usually end?" I asked him. I knew I was being a royal bitch this morning, but I couldn't stop myself. I was so hurt by the way he'd betrayed me and betrayed my trust. It was a defense mechanism I couldn't put a lid on.

Elijah tilted his head in that perfectly sexy way that usually drove me insane.

But not this time. I rolled my eyes and looked out the window to my right. He was lucky I didn't punch him in the face.

"What do you mean?"

With a scowl, I said, "Give me a break, Banks. You're not a dense man."

"No, seriously, Hannah. Enlighten me. Right now, I'm

not going to take anything for granted when it comes to understanding you. What are you asking me?"

I exhaled loudly and let my shoulders drop. God, I was exhausted. "I was wondering if all your breakups ended with one person hating the other." After I finished the comment, I continued to glare at him.

Subtly he moved his head left to right. Left to right again. The gesture looked more like disbelief than a negative answer. "I haven't had a relationship since that witch we saw at the courthouse. I swore I would never be hurt by a woman again. I would never trust a woman again." His voice was raw with emotion, and for the first time all morning, it affected me.

We stared at each other for much too long until I felt like my heart was in danger of freezing over from looking into those damn icy-green eyes. He looked so hurt. As hurt as I felt. And so lost. I wasn't sure we'd be able to find our way back.

Christ, how did we get here?

"Where do you want me to take you?" Elijah asked flatly, seeming to have found new resolve after that last exchange.

Fascinated with the view out my window—fine, *pretending* to be fascinated with the view out my window, I answered, "I'll get my car and some things from your house. I can send someone for the rest later."

"All right," he said quietly, looked over his left shoulder, and waited for an opportunity to pull back into traffic.

The rest of the drive was made in the loudest silence I'd ever endured. By the time he turned onto his street in Malibu, I wanted to dive out of the car and run on my own two feet the last stretch of the way. My silver BMW sat right where I'd parked it. He must have really tied one on last night not to have noticed it there. I had to bite into the inside of my cheek not to make a comment of the sort.

I followed him through the front gate and along the walk to the front door, keeping several paces behind him. It reminded me so much of my first days here with him. He had given me a list of rules to follow, and I'd thought he was an egomaniac asshole.

Hey, what do you know? My mom always taught me to trust my first impression of a person.

"I'll just be a few minutes, and then I'll be out of your way. No matter what's happened between us over the past few days, I will always cherish the other memories I made here with you. I just want to tell you that. Goodbye, Elijah."

When he began to speak, I just held up my flat hand to gesture *Stop*. Enough had been said and done already. I was being honest. I really did have beautiful memories here, and I didn't want them all to be tarnished.

I hurried down the long hall to the master bedroom and riffled through the section of the large walk-in closet where my stuff was hanging. Quickly, I started yanking things down from the hangers. Shirt, shirt, jeans, chef jacket, another one, and then I dropped to my knees to grab my work shoes, a pair of sneakers, and my Uggs. That was all I could carry, so that was all I would take. I'd have to send my dad back for the rest.

Shit, that was going to be a great conversation.

Well, that did it. For some reason, the thought of telling my dad about another failed relationship cracked me straight down the middle. I completely fell apart on the floor of the massive walk-in closet, clutching my clothes and shoes like a teenage runaway.

While surrounded by Elijah's thousand-dollar dress shirts and high-end business suits, my broken heart betrayed me in messy sobs and hiccupping gasps. I buried my face in my clothes so I wouldn't be heard and tried desperately to pull myself together.

But the events of the previous night came flooding back into my mind. And now those memories were holding hands with my old friend anxiety. I wiped my eyes with trembling hands, but it was no use. The tears were coming faster than I could rub them away.

"A… My n-n-aaame is Ann-na. My h-h-usban-d's n-name is A-d-um. Wee"—*sniff*—"come fr-rom Amm-ster-dam." I exhaled slowly through pressed lips. "A-an-dd we s-s-sell ap-pp-les."

I rocked back and forth on my bent knees and inhaled through my nose. I was desperate to stave off this attack. This was an oldie but goody right here. A trick my therapist taught me when I was just a girl, and I never stopped using it. Talking out loud regulated my breathing pattern, and thinking of what to say for each letter preoccupied my mind.

So, I moved on to the letter *b*. I was on *f* when I was calm enough to notice Elijah standing in the doorway looking twelve kinds of scared and helpless.

"Baby, can I help you?" He dropped down to his knees too, and I started crying again. Goddammit, just when I'd gotten it under control.

"All right, all right," he crooned, pulling my clothes out from between us. "Come to me."

He held out his arms, and I wanted to crawl into them more than anything in this world. I wanted it so bad.

This was where the dominant man took over. He pulled me into his chest and held me as close as two people could be without being joined during lovemaking. I gave in to the safety and comfort I was so hungry for and melted into him. The warmth of his body against mine was finally doing some good against the chill I couldn't shake from being outside all night. I was so grateful it was still summer, or those early dawn hours would have been unbearably cold.

More tears. More shudders. More sniffles and sobs. I couldn't stop any of it no matter how hard I tried, and Elijah softly whispered beautiful words to me the whole time. While I heard what he said, I only let them penetrate so deep. Never again would I let his words, or any man's words, into my heart. This pain was much too great to bear. How would I survive this? This betrayal was too much.

With all that fuel behind me, I pushed back from him. The anger came rushing in again as fierce as it ever had.

"Stop this." I shoved at his chest to try to get out of his embrace.

But this time, he had his steel-band arms locked around me, holding me against him. Since we were already on the ground, his most vulnerable spots weren't the easy target they would have been if we had been standing.

"No. *You* stop this," he growled, and his voice was deeper and had a sinister edge I couldn't remember hearing. On him or any other human.

In some combination of lightning-fast moves, the bastard joined our hands together with a set of metal handcuffs. I looked down and tugged on the device, pulling his arm along with mine so I could inspect the entrapment closer.

"Hey, do you mind?" he asked in a snarky tone and pulled his arm back, this time yanking mine closer to him.

"Take these off immediately," I demanded with death-ray eyes.

"No. In fact..." He walked swiftly toward the bathroom, dragging me with him.

"No, I don't need to watch you pee," I protested. "Thank you, though." I hooked my arm around the open doorway of the linen closet as we scurried by. He was moving us along at a good enough pace, though, and I couldn't anchor myself in time and stumbled after him anyway.

But instead of using the toilet, he held the little key between our faces.

"We're going to work out whatever is going on here or take each other apart, piece by piece." Elijah waggled his brows and tilted his head a bit. His hair flopped over to the side, and he gave me a slow, sexy grin. "That might be fun. You know?"

He dropped the key into the toilet and flushed with his free hand before I could even process what was happening.

"You fucking idiot. Tell me you have another key. How am I going to work like this? Or drive, or shower? My God, what were you thinking?" I was yelling by the time I finished and really didn't care. That was so irresponsible.

"Language, lady. You're out of hand today."

After he issued that little reprimand, he started walking toward the door of the bedroom.

"Hey! You can't just pull me along behind you everywhere."

As he did just that, I found myself talking to his back. At least the view was lovely. Down the hall toward the kitchen we went, his arm fully extended behind him and mine out in front of me.

"How are we going to get these off?" I hurried to catch up to my hand to see the lock. Maybe I could pick the thing with a bobby pin or paper clip. Didn't they do that on television?

Elijah put his hand over the cuff. "Forget it, beauty. They're tamperproof. I don't mess around with toys. You know that."

I just stared at him. My God, he was infuriating. And gorgeous. And so damn pretty to look at that it sometimes took my breath away. When I realized he was locked in the stare too, I quickly turned my head. This man was too good at reading me, and I'd already given him the intimacy of my mind and body.

"I'm hungry," he announced to no one in particular.

Or maybe it was to me. I couldn't be sure. But if he thought I was cooking for him, he was more delusional than I imagined. Not to mention, he never spoke to me like a demanding caveman. And I'd be damned if it was something I'd start responding to now.

"All right, I'm going to head out, then. I just need to get that stuff I left on the floor."

I intentionally used the hand tethered to his to thumb over my shoulder, yanking his along with mine. I gave this ridiculous experiment two hours at the most before he got tired of it and took these things off.

"Hannah," he sighed and dramatically dropped his chin to his chest.

"Yes?" I asked with impatience.

"Clearly, you're not going anywhere. Not until we get to the bottom of what's going on here between us. How can you just throw this away?" He motioned between our two bodies. "Throw *us* away?"

"See, now that's funny. Right there." I poked my index finger into his shoulder and continued. "That's so funny you are saying that."

"I wasn't trying to be funny. Help me understand. I know I never told you I suspected I had a child. Admittedly, that's a huge detail to omit from someone's story. It's not something I talk about because it's very painful. Up until that day in that courthouse, I had given up on the notion of ever even confirming or denying the child was mine. Because she disappeared."

He made a gesture with his hands, of course yanking mine along with his, like a small explosion between our faces.

"*Poof,* here one day, gone the next. For five months, she led me to believe that my child was growing inside her, and we were planning for a family and a life together. And then one day she stood by our front door with all her bags packed and announced, 'Oh, just kidding, the baby isn't yours, and I'm in love with someone else,' and left. She just left."

I didn't know what to say. Really, what would you say to that? I witnessed the emotional damage that woman had done to this loving, generous, giving man. If he didn't harbor all the resentment and animosity toward womankind in general because of Hensley, I couldn't imagine the full-force boyfriend he would be. Really, if this was him holding back, he'd be downright scary at full tilt.

"I'm sorry you were treated that way. I know she caused you a lot of pain and continues to affect your relationships." There. That was fair and kind. I couldn't be faulted for an answer like that.

"Will you have a paternity test done now that you know where to find her? Does she still have custody of the child?" I asked and then wanted to retract the question just as fast. First of all, it was terribly rude. Secondly, and probably mostly, I wasn't sure I wanted to know the answer. Did he plan on reuniting with that woman? If the child was his, were they going to run back into each other's arms and make a happy family?

That thought made my gut roil, and I sneaked a peek over to the sink to see if it was empty in case I had to lose my stomach's contents.

I held my free hand up as if to say *Stop*. "You know what? Not my business."

"Please don't say that."

"Why? Why would you want me grilling you like that? It's not fair of me, not at all. I'm tired and emotional, and I have to readjust to the way things are now. I have no right to ask you things like that. I have no right to ask you anything, frankly."

"What is this about? You keep saying things as if we're over." He put his strong hands on my hips and pulled me against him. "Is that what all of this is about? Just level with me, Hannah. Are you breaking up with me because of the way I acted at the courthouse?"

I stared up into his beautiful face. His hypnotic eyes were full of anguish, and none of it made sense. None of it. When I tried to push away from him, he held on tighter.

"No. Tell me where we stand. Let's do this like adults. I want to know what's going on, straight up. I've been trying to guess for the past three hours, and I'm no closer to figuring it out."

"You had to have known," I said, glaring at him. How could he be acting so clueless? He had to have known what would happen to me when I walked onto that jobsite.

"Known what? In fact, just assume I don't know. Because right now, I really don't know anything."

The more he spoke, the more I wondered if I had something wrong. Either this was one giant mix-up, or he was an outstanding liar and all the carrying on about disliking liars was just that, carrying on.

"When you told me to meet you last night at Shark's Edge, what did you think would happen?"

"What?" Elijah twisted his face in confusion. "When I what?" His voice went higher with each question, and I rolled my eyes at his dramatics.

"Please don't patronize me." I sighed.

"I'm not patronizing you. But I'm also not understanding you. I didn't tell you to meet me at Shark's Edge last night. Why would I do that? Why would I tell you to meet me at a jobsite? In the dark?"

Now the tone of incredulousness he was taking with me was pissing me off. Like I was the dumb one here.

"I don't know. It didn't make sense to me either. But the text message came from your phone number. You've admitted to me, more than once this morning, that you drank too much last night. Is there a chance you did it and don't remember?"

"Here. Look at my phone. You'll see I didn't send you a message telling you to meet me there." In a hurry, he pulled out his phone and slapped it on the counter. He scrolled back to last night, and what do you know? Right there it was.

"I did not send that. What is all of this? I was with Bas and Grant at this time. They can vouch for me. And also that I didn't leave to go to meet you at the Edge."

"Oh, trust me, I know you didn't show up. But three other guys did." Ahh, there was the bit of information that got him to freeze in his tracks. His little tirade came to a quick halt when I threw out that detail.

With an ashen face and meek voice, he asked, "What?"

"Do I really have to repeat that?" I bit back.

In a blink, his color flushed back into his cheeks, and his tone became lethal. "Hannah? Did they hurt you?"

And then he switched to careful and concerned. "Beautiful girl. I'm so sorry this happened, but I swear I didn't send those texts to you."

This was like watching someone change Halloween masks, but their entire personality changed instead.

"I would never lead you to a dangerous place like that. Ever. You have to believe me. If for no other reason, base that knowledge on the time we've spent together. I've always taken your safety seriously, have I not?"

I was so damn confused, I didn't know which end was up. And I'd seen him play this tactic before, so no, I didn't exactly trust him. God, that stabbed my own heart to admit that to myself.

But the facts were right in front of us. So my temper flared again. "Why are those messages on your phone, then?" I shouted, and frankly, it felt good.

"It wasn't me!"

"Don't you fucking shout at me right now, mister. I barely escaped a gang rape last night because you led me into some fucked-up situation. And for what? I can't seem to figure that out. Maybe just for kicks? See how many women you can get to do your bidding, or ensure you still have control over me at least? Maybe seeing the old flame reminded you that at least one of your old fucks had the strength to break your magic spell and get away from you."

Elijah stared at me for long seconds after that. And then a few more.

"What?" I snapped.

"I've just never seen this side of you. I don't really know what to make of it. It's frightening and fascinating all at the same time. Just when you think you know someone, and then something like this—" He waved his free hand up and down the length of my body like he was showing off a prize cow at the state fair.

I sincerely considered kneeing him in the balls like I had the one guy last night.

"So what happened when you got to the jobsite?"

"Isn't it obvious?" I scowled, really not wanting to have to give him a blow-by-blow account of the situation.

"No. Tell me what happened."

"You texted me and told me where to meet you specifically—"

"It wasn't me texting you. Obviously, someone commandeered my VPN or something. I'll have to dig into that." He motioned wildly with his hand. "But go on."

"When I got to where I thought you would be and you weren't there, I started to really get nervous. I had pepper spray in my bag, so I had that at the ready, and this man came up behind me and scared the crap out of me. He knew my name and everything." My breathing was starting to labor, so I closed my eyes and took a few moments to center myself again.

Elijah was patient now because he had gotten used to these exercises I went through when agitated to stave off a full-blown attack.

After I reengaged in our conversation, he asked, "Did you get a good look at him?"

"Pretty good, yeah. I mean, it was dark, but there was enough light from the places they are currently working, you know? I even snapped shots of them after I pepper sprayed them, but I don't know where my phone is now."

"Okay, that's really good. Do you think you can work with someone on a sketch?"

"Yes, probably. But Elijah, I don't think it will do much good. They got away and ran off long before Mr. Cole found me there."

"Did they touch you? At all—anywhere?"

"No. They would have. They were disgusting." I shivered involuntarily just thinking about their smell and the way the one leered at me.

"How many were there?" Elijah asked next.

I was beginning to feel like I was being questioned by law enforcement. His questions were coming one after the other.

"Three that I saw."

"Did they ask you for anything? Money... information?"

"No, they said their boss wanted them to get me and bring me to him. I kind of lost it when I heard that. I know the statistics from the situation when I was young. If you are taken from the scene, your chance of not being found increases dramatically."

The gorgeous man pulled me into him and held me there. It might have been for his own comfort—it might have been for mine. We both needed physical reassurance in that moment, so we clung onto each other and said nothing for long minutes. I could feel him inhaling the scent of my hair repeatedly as if memorizing fine details to hold sacred after I left. Maybe I was making that part up, but I wanted to believe he'd be that devastated if I left.

Finally, Elijah asked, "So how did you get away? From three men?"

"I used my pepper spray on two, and one I kneed in the groin. One had a broken shoelace, so his boot wasn't tied well." My hands were telling the story as much as my words, so Elijah's hand was getting yanked along for the ride. He teased me about talking with my hands all the time, so his grin was extra wide now that he was an active participant in my habit.

"I knew he should be the one left standing if I had to leave one upright. It made sense, right? He wouldn't be able to run fast with a boot flopping all around." I finally finished and rested my hands on the island.

"You are so smart. I'm so proud of you." Elijah hugged me close to his chest again. This time he kissed my forehead, but it was very parental. "That was really fast thinking."

"I was able to outrun him and duck under the staircase. I was so scared to move until Mr. Cole found me there this morning." I finished my tale from his embrace, and he looked awestruck.

"My God. My beautiful baby. I promise you I will find out who did this, and they will pay for this. No one fucks with what's mine."

The moment those words left his lips, I was shaking my head. "Like I told you earlier, I'm not your burden, Elijah."

"Cut the bullshit, Hannah. You're right. You're not a burden. You're the woman I love. There's a big difference." He stared at me with challenge on every feature, all but daring me to argue with him on the point.

"You love me?"

"Yes. With all my heart. You're driving me a little batshit crazy today, but yes, I love you," he said with the widest grin.

"I'm so confused."

"Well, Han, your attitude has been atrocious."

I pushed his shoulder. "Not about that."

"What, then?"

"You had to have known how dangerous that situation was that you led me into. I don't know if you were using me as bait or what?" I shook my head, trying to make sense of the situation compared to his words now, and it just didn't add up.

"Woman, listen to me. I did not send you those text messages. There is technology to make it look like I did, but I did not. You must believe me. I've never lied to you before, have I?"

He stared at me expectantly as I turned over his words.

Ask him who he had dinner with last night.

"No, not that I know of, at least." Then it hit me like a freight train. How had I not seen this before? "Were those the same guys who kidnapped Grant? Off the boat he and Rio were on?"

He thought for a moment and finally said, "The only way we're going to know that is by getting you, Grant, and Rio together in the same room to compare notes. The timing on that will be up to you since you're fresh off the ordeal. Do you want to take a shower? A nap? Are you hungry?"

I lifted my hand to rub my forehead and dragged his hand with mine. "Please take these off. This is ridiculous."

"No can do. I really don't have another key."

"You're a fucking idiot. What were you thinking?" How were we going to live like this?

That trademark grin spread across his face again. "Well, I can think of a few positives about this arrangement."

I, on the other hand, saw nothing to be smiling about. "Really? Enlighten me."

"Well, for one thing, you won't be going anywhere without me, so I can ensure your safety. Also, you'll still be sleeping in the same bed as me. Not to mention, looks like we'll be showering together. We've always had fun in the shower, haven't we?"

He had the nerve to look hopeful and, goddammit, sexy while saying that. Or maybe it was the idea and the memories that were sexy and not the man himself. Or all three?

"Can I use your cell phone, please? I'm going to need to replace mine as soon as possible."

"Who do you need to call?" he asked nonchalantly but didn't hand over his phone.

"Is it really your business?"

"If you're going to be making the call from my cell phone it is."

"You can't just hold me here hostage. I want to call a locksmith to get these fucking things off us, and then I'm going to leave here, replace my phone, and go home and decide what I need to do from there."

He looked like I just kicked his shins and stole his favorite toy. "So you still want to leave? After everything I explained to you?"

"Do you remember, not that long ago, I was going to move back to my parents' house? When everything was going just fine between us, I still intended on moving back to their place. I should have done it then. We need to get space between us. We jumped into this relationship thing too fast. We don't know each other well enough to be living together. I shouldn't be blindsided when skeletons fall out of your closet like I was in front of the courthouse."

"How long are you going to hold my past against me? I don't do that to you. Our past makes us who we are today. Not to weaponize in an argument or when you feel insecure about our relationship advancing too quickly."

"That's not what I'm doing. That's absurd."

"Is it?"

"Elijah, listen to me. I'm not using your past against you. Try to look at this from my point of view and be honest with me about it. How would it feel to see me hysterical—" I put up my hand to stop him from interrupting, because he sharply inhaled to do just that. I gave him a sideways warning stare before continuing. "How would it feel to see me hysterical when I saw an ex-boyfriend? And not a fresh breakup, but one from yeeeeaars ago that rewired my entire mind-set on relationships, dating, and the general existence of an entire gender?"

I stopped him from answering again because this was too important to just fly off the handle with the first knee-jerk response that came to him. He should really contemplate his answer here.

"No, don't spout off on this. It's too crucial to our future. I think it's worth sitting with for a moment. I mean really be present"—I swirled my hand around in front of his face like I was washing a window between us—"with all of that for a little while and see how it feels. God knows I just had that opportunity all night and into the early morning hours. It's only fair."

Not thinking, I turned to walk away and give him some privacy and was immediately yanked back by our joined hands.

"Goddammit." I grumbled a few more choice words and sank down onto one of the stools at the island. Burying my face in my folded arms, exhaustion overtook me. A nap felt possible sitting right where I was.

"Come on, baby." Elijah's voice was right beside my ear. The proximity startled me, and I jumped, but he held me close to his body as he carried me down the hall.

"Wait. Where are you—no, put me down." I tried to push

away from his chest, but his strength was no match for me, especially given how tired I felt.

"Why must you fight me on everything? You're exhausted. Let's just lie down for a while so you can rest." He spoke gently as he laid me on the bed.

The heavy drapes were still closed from the night before, and my lids were impossible to keep open as soon as I felt the pillow beneath my head.

"Do you want the covers pulled up?" my caretaker asked quietly.

"Yes, please," I grumbled into the pillow as he spooned in behind me to rest our joined hands across my abdomen. Good thing we didn't mind sleeping this way.

I was out before I could give it another thought. All I could hope for when I woke was some sort of clarity about where he and I stood and a freaking key to unlock the cuff that bound me to him physically.

The bigger problem was that he held my heart prisoner too. Breaking free from that captivity would take a lot more time and effort, if I could escape his hold at all.

CHAPTER ELEVEN

ELIJAH

Propped on one elbow, I watched Hannah sleep for hours. I was so lost to this woman and now feared I was going to lose her. How had this all turned so sideways?

She'd left me with a lot to think about, and out of respect to her and to the relationship I wanted desperately to salvage, that was all I had done since she fell asleep beside me. So with every cycle of breath she took, in and out, in and out, my heart felt like a little piece blew away. I pictured a heart-shaped dandelion pouf with wispy seedlings blowing away in the breeze. Although, when it was your heart deteriorating, it wasn't nearly as peaceful.

It was hard to know where to go from here. I acknowledged my behavior was out of line yesterday. I wasn't sure what more I could do.

My reaction yesterday was nothing but shock and frustration. It wasn't passion or lost love found again like she had herself believing. It was anger and betrayal, just like it was every time I thought of that woman. But I already knew what Hannah would say. The fact that I could have such a strong emotional reaction to her meant I still had strong emotions for her. Totally calling bullshit on that one.

I toyed with the ends of her blond hair, and she sighed

a bit louder. She had been sleeping for three hours, and even though I really had to use the bathroom, I didn't want to wake her. I would suffer eight nights of discomfort if it meant she was well rested.

How did she not know how much I cared about her at this point? Why had she looked surprised when I told her I loved her? That seemed preposterous to me. I felt like I was showing her day in and day out with my actions and my words and especially with my body how much I cared about her, needed her, and wanted her. Yet she'd looked at me like I had lost my damn mind when I said she was the woman I loved.

Hannah Farsey was by far the most confusing woman I had ever met. That was a large part of my attraction to her. The intrigue. The curiosity. The excitement of not knowing what would be around the next bend.

Her unpredictability was usually a good thing. It kept my day exciting. Her spirit was youthful and energetic, and she never seemed to be weighed down with life getting too heavy. Was I doing that to her now? Was I bringing all those negative things into her world? Because the woman lying beside me was not the same woman who took me in a hot-air balloon early one Saturday morning. The gleam in her eye that day was brighter than the new day's sun, and I was more excited that morning to see what life had in store for us as a couple than I had been about anything since the disaster with Hensley.

Finally, I'd thought to myself that morning as we glided over the coast, I'd paid my dues. It was time for me to be happy again. But I should have known better...

Because there was more to the animosity toward Hensley Pritchett than even my best friends knew. She carried my deepest, darkest secret with her. She had the power to level me in all ways—physically, emotionally, and legally.

It was time for me to come to a decision. Because if I didn't, I was going to lose Hannah, and that would destroy me. If the incredible creature I held in my arms left me, I'd have no reason to live. Hensley could have open season. She could tell everyone what she knew about me. It wouldn't matter anymore. But if I told them first, I could control the narrative, and there was a good chance I could save this relationship... and hopefully save myself.

God, I wasn't sure I was strong enough to do it. I would be putting myself at major risk of going to prison, and then what was it all for? Hannah would be alone anyway because I would be locked up. Sebastian would have a public relations nightmare on his hands—again. That was the last thing he and his new family needed to deal with.

Before I overthought this and talked myself out of doing it, I needed to call Sebastian and Grant and have them come over. We needed to have a long talk, and it needed to be in private. With my free hand, I sent our three-way chat a text message.

Need to talk to you both. Malibu?

Bas answered first.

Some of us are working. Remember that thing called your job?

Grant was more considerate, of course.

You okay, my man? What's going on?

Just come when you can,
but come together so I only have
to say all of this once. Please.

I made sure my phone was on silent and tossed it onto the mattress facedown. It didn't matter how they responded at that point, and the banter could go on for the next half hour with those two. I'd see them when they got here, and finally, after all these years of living in fear of my tea being spilled, I would purge these demons that were eating me up inside.

It would be better this way.

I just had to keep telling myself that.

At least Hannah was handcuffed to me and wouldn't be able to run out. I'd keep the spare key hidden a bit longer.

Yes, I had one, regardless of what I'd been telling her. Did that make me an asshole? Maybe. Desperate times called for desperate measures and all that. I was definitely a desperate man and wasn't proud of any of this bullshit. But in the end, I'd gotten her to hear me out, so that was a win.

Another hour passed, and Hannah finally rolled to her back. It took her a few minutes to focus tired eyes and remember where she was. With a sullen groan, she lifted her hands to rub her face, and mine went with hers, reminding her of that situation too.

"For Christ's sake, Elijah!" she shouted, and I jumped from the outburst. "Take this off. Enough already."

"I'll have to call someone in, beautiful. But if you don't mind, I really have to piss."

"Ugh, this ridiculous," she groused, but we got up together and went to the toilet.

"Ladies first," I offered with a sweep of my hand, trying to do the gentlemanly thing.

"I'm never going to be able to go with you standing there. I already know this will never happen."

"Then let me in there because I'll have no problem, and I've been holding it for about three hours. No, longer, actually."

"Why didn't you just wake me?" she asked from the farthest point away she could stretch our arms. She could stand outside the room while I used it at least.

"You could sit backward," I offered.

"What?"

"Think about it. If you sit backward, it will be like me standing here, so I will be out there. Is that enough privacy to go?" When she didn't reject the idea immediately, I took it as a good sign. "Let's try it, at least."

"I'm never going to forgive you for this," she bitched while using both hands to unfasten her jeans and shimmy them down her thighs. Having my hands so close to her bare skin was too tempting not to reach out and touch her.

"Don't get any ideas," Hannah warned as she sat down. "Now go out like I did, please." She continued muttering to herself while I stood as far away as possible. This gig was going to be up the minute the bathroom situation took a more serious turn. For either one of us, if I were honest.

My beautiful girl finished, and we both washed our hands. I couldn't take my eyes off her while she lathered up and scrubbed. How did something so ordinary become so fascinating when she did it? It was the careful and meticulous way she went about everything. She didn't splash water outside the basin or get soap suds on her sleeve. When we rinsed, the water was just the right temperature. She was a perfectionist through and through, but not to the extent that it ruined her day if things didn't go perfectly.

It made me wonder out loud, "Were you like this when you were a little girl?"

She sighed heavily and stared at me. "Like what?" she finally gave in and asked with no patience gained from her rest.

"Careful. Precise. I don't know…" I shrugged. I really wasn't looking for an argument.

A small smile tugged the side of her mouth, and she answered, "My mom says I came out of the womb and organized the doctor's bag for her. So yes, apparently, I was born this way. Something about order calms me. Chaos makes me…" She thought for a moment before saying, "I don't know, chaotic inside. I feel anxious when things aren't in order. It was an easy transition moving in here with you because you are very tidy and organized. Almost unusually so for a man. Don't you think?"

"Possibly. But you know, guys don't sit around talking about alphabetizing their spice rack. So, it's hard to know just how many do it." I had to laugh when picturing Sebastian doing something like that. Although if Abbigail told him to do it, he'd do the chore with a smile on his face if it meant he was making his woman happy.

As we stood talking in the middle of the bathroom, I was hit with an intense wave of panic. I felt the color drain from my face and stall in my heart, where the damn thing was swelling to an unnatural size in my chest. And fuck, did it hurt. Hurt to the point I couldn't breathe. First, I rubbed the center of my chest, but that didn't touch it. Not even close. My vision blurred, and the room alternated between tipping this way and that and spinning.

"Hey, hey there." Hannah's voice came to me, but I couldn't

tell from where. "Hey, baby, let's sit down, right here. Sit down with me, Elijah, or you're going to really hurt yourself."

I must have done what she wanted, because I heard her saying, "That's better. Good. Close your eyes for a little bit, and let's get some blood back to the rest of your body."

I could feel her stroking her fingers through my hair, and it was so nice. Over and over again until I finally opened my eyes to find we were on the floor of my bathroom.

"What the hell?" I mumbled.

"Ssshhh..." Hannah said in a whisper. "Stay a few more minutes. You almost passed out. Let's make sure it's fully gone before you stand up again."

"That was the strangest thing. I don't know—"

She cut me off again with another long "Ssshhhhh..." And it felt so divine to be in her care, I just did what she said. She was going to make a perfect mother someday.

"Do you want children?" I asked out of nowhere. Of course I knew the train of thought that led me to pull into this station, but to her, it must have seemed out of the blue.

"Yes, of course. Although at this rate..." She cut herself off midsentence.

I sat up slowly to make sure the floor didn't fall out from under me. "At this rate what? What were you going to say?" I prodded.

"It doesn't matter. Are you feeling better? Do you want to try to stand? You scared me there for a moment."

"Don't change the subject, please. I feel like what you were going to say was important."

"No, it's not. What's important is what made you get so faint? Are you still hungover?"

"Nah, that's long gone. Can we sit down and talk, though?

But maybe not here in the bathroom?"

"All right. Afterward, we really need to call a locksmith to come get these dumb handcuffs off so I can leave."

Damn, I thought she would've let up on that idea after getting some rest. I'd worry about it after Grant and Bas left. We sat down on the sofa in the bedroom, and I took both her hands in mine. Nothing changed about me wanting to be touching her whenever she was near.

"So what did you want to talk about?" She stared at me expectantly. While some of the sourness was gone from her attitude, she still wasn't her usual gentle, loving self.

"When we were in the bathroom just now, I had an overwhelming sensation of panic or dread. Hell, I don't know. Does that sound dramatic?"

I waited for some sort of answer from her.

"No, of course not. You're talking to the girl who lives with an anxiety disorder on a daily basis, Elijah. No, it doesn't sound dramatic in the least."

That comment caused her expression to become sad, or maybe desolate was a better descriptor. She'd explained to me once before that she sometimes felt completely alone in a crowded room. That her mental health stuff made her feel so isolated, and it broke my heart then, too.

"I was trying to imagine every day here without you, and it hurt so badly. It physically hurt me." I touched the center of my chest. "I couldn't breathe, and my heart felt like it was grinding gears. I don't know how to explain it . . . but it was a feeling I've never felt before, and it scared me."

Hannah listened intently but didn't offer much of a response. She couldn't maintain eye contact with me either, and I didn't know what to make of that. From what I knew of her, she was always very direct and engaged when she talked to me.

"What are you thinking right now? What's going through your mind? Is all that freaking you out?" Internally, I rolled my eyes at my word choice. The dreaded *what are you thinking?*

She squeezed my hands in hers. "No, you're not freaking me out. I'm so confused. I don't want to be a fool, you know? I don't want to be played, and no offense, but you have quite the reputation of being a player, Mr. Banks."

The smile I gave her didn't reach my eyes. There was no way it could have because it wasn't sincere. It was just to let her off the hook for feeling bad. I knew what people said about me, and I didn't care. I intentionally worked on that reputation. I wanted people to think I was shallow. Especially women. That way, they would never expect to develop a relationship with me—and eventually get hurt by me.

Because that was what inevitably happened to everyone I loved. I hurt them.

"No matter what I say here, it's going to sound like I'm trying to dazzle you with bullshit, but I'm not. I've told you before, including several times today, that you are the exception, not the rule. I want to be with you, build a life with you."

"But I saw the way you reacted to seeing your ex. No matter what you say, that is not the way someone who is over their feelings for another person behaves. Maybe we need to just take a break..." The tears that were welling in her eyes finally spilled over and rolled down her cheeks one after the other.

But my brave girl soldiered on. "And you resolve your issues with that woman. You can find out if the child is yours, or whatever, and come back to me when I can have all of you." Hannah wiped her cheeks with the sleeve of her shirt, and tears replaced the others immediately. "Because I deserve that. I deserve all of someone. Not another woman's leftovers."

With hideous or perfect timing—I couldn't decide right then—my doorbell rang. Bas and Grant were the only guests I was expecting. In light of what just happened the previous night, I pulled up the security app on my phone and checked the camera aimed at the front door to be sure it was them.

As suspected, my two best friends stood impatiently waiting for me to disengage the lock. I punched in the code on my phone and explained to Hannah that I asked them to come over. She assumed it was to fill them in on what happened last night at the Edge jobsite, and she was partially correct. The three of them had no idea the bomb I was about to drop on them.

She and I made our way out to the front door just as they were coming in.

"Hey, guys, thanks for coming over." I stuck my hand out to Grant first, and we shook awkwardly since my other hand was tethered to Hannah.

Grant noticed immediately since he and I had an elaborate handshake we always executed.

"Well, don't let us get in the way of your kinky shenanigans," the tall guy joked.

Hannah was the first to squash the illusion. "It's not what it looks like."

Little did she know, a comment like that just scented them on her trail harder.

Grant gave a sly grin. "Mmm-hmm. That's what they all say."

Sebastian was already antsy and wanting to get down to business. "What can we do for you, Banks? You wanted us here, you got us here. Spill it."

"Can I get anybody a drink?" I asked my guests.

"Oh, no, don't get him started on the drink service again," Bas muttered to Grant, and I wanted to pop him. I wasn't in the mood for their shit today.

"Hannah was attacked last night at the Edge jobsite." There. That should shut down the Laurel and Hardy routine.

"Come again?" Bas said.

"Well, that explains the cuffs. Feeling a bit possessive, are we?" Grant grinned, and I thought there was an actual twinkle in his eye. He would love to see me move on from my past more than anyone.

"Fuck off," I growled. "Like you'd do anything different."

He just held his hands up in supplication because he knew I was one hundred percent accurate.

"Where's the key?"

"What does it matter? Why is that the first thing you're asking me?"

"Planning purposes. If we're moving them all out, I may need to employ a similar maneuver. We all have our hands full, you know?"

"I flushed it."

My two best friends threw their heads back with laughter. But they sobered up quick because they were also aware that we had some serious shit to deal with. And as most things went, what involved one of us usually involved us all.

For the next hour, Hannah retold her account of what happened the night before. As I promised, both men vouched for my whereabouts when those text messages were sent from my phone, and the three of us came up with a plan on who we knew that could do forensics on my phone without destroying the device. Mostly because that was the way these bastards thought they were controlling us at the moment, so we could use their own tactics against them.

I went to my stash and grabbed one of the extra phones I kept on hand and gave them both the number. Hannah still insisted on getting her own new phone and not using one of mine, and it just wasn't the hill I was going to die on today, so I let it go.

"So where does that leave us?" I asked the two of them. "We need a game plan, because I'm not going to have her attacked again. Thank God she got away from them this time. Grant, does that sound like the same guys who came aboard your yacht and took you?"

Grant focused on Hannah for a second or two before asking, "Did you say the one guy had a couple of teeth missing?"

She nodded before saying, "Yes, I'm sure of it. It was dark but light enough from where they're working currently. You know what I mean? The light spills over?"

"Sure, sure," Bas contributed. "They're really bright lights."

"And as much as I hate to bring it up again, because I remember what happened last time, but Hannah mentioned how bad the men smelled."

As soon as I said the words, she pinched her face and recoiled.

Grant closed his eyes and began some sort of counting exercise, and Bas and I made eye contact with one another and then bugged our eyes wider like *what the hell are we watching right now?*

"Of course, there could be other criminals with missing teeth that smell bad, but I thought the bit about bringing you guys to their boss seemed familiar too," I stated, trying to move away from the odor conversation.

"Yeah, I don't know why I was never taken to this boss they kept talking about," said Grant. "I think the cargo we were carrying was getting way past its due date, if you pick up what I'm laying down, and they ran out of time. So they dumped me first and the rest as soon as they got rid of me."

Hannah looked puzzled and asked Grant directly, "What cargo were they carrying?"

Bas pinched the bridge of his nose and mumbled, "Oh, Christ, here we go."

Grant shot a glare my way. Through clenched teeth, he said, "You didn't tell her? I thought we were telling the girls?"

Now I was pissed because this was going to look like another thing I was keeping from her, just when I was making a little headway with her before they got here.

"No, you and Bas were telling Rio and Abbigail because they were directly involved at that point. Hannah was not. But now she is, so now I have to tell her the rest of this fucked-up shit so she can have nightmares about it too!" I was yelling and waving my hands around, yanking my poor girl back and forth where we were connected.

When I looked at her angelic face, I was devastated. All the trust that used to be there was now disdain and accusation. Any hope of love was betrayal and disbelief. Any dreams of a future and a family were as dead as the bodies in the cargo hold of that pirate ship.

"Fuck this shit!" I bellowed.

Labored breathing and off-the-charts frustration

contorted my face into something either unrecognizable or straight-up frightening judging by the way everyone in the room stared at me.

I could feel my chest heaving in and out with each greedy gulp of air, but the combination of panic and anger was a bizarre cocktail I wasn't used to, and I was having trouble regulating my body and my expression.

"All right, big guy." Grant stood in front of me and put his hands on my shoulders.

I let my head hang forward until my chin touched my chest and stayed there while I tried to calm down.

"That's good. Breathe," he said in a soothing voice. A stray thought in the back of my brain wondered if these were techniques he picked up from having to deal with his crazy girlfriend all the time.

Great. That's the category I'm getting lumped into now.

Finally, I raised my gaze to meet his. With him standing so close, that meant I had to tilt my head back and look up a few inches. I was of decent height, but this guy … this guy was ridiculous.

A slow grin moved across my mouth and then his too.

"You can take your hands off me now, chief," I teased him.

He gave my shoulders a squeeze and said, "But you're just so muscular." He fluttered his eyelids in faux rapture. "I can't help it."

In my periphery, I saw Hannah observing our banter and not knowing what to make of it. I realized most of the time she and I had been together, we'd spent it alone. She didn't realize how close my relationship was with these two men. I mean, I'd told her stories and tried to explain in words, but nothing got the point across like observing the behavior for herself.

She surprised me by piping up next. "Are the girls coming? Rio and Abby, I mean?"

Grant stepped back from me and said, "That reminds me. I'm supposed to find out where Kendall is. I didn't see her on the street or in the driveway. Where is Rio's car? She wanted me to bring it home if it was here."

"Oh no," Hannah whimpered in despair and dropped her head into her hands, pulling mine with hers.

"What is it, baby?" I asked with concern while rubbing her back with my free hand.

I still thought the benefits of this cuffing outweighed the drawbacks.

"Rio's car," she answered from behind the shield of her hands.

"What about it? Did you have it?" I asked in a calm voice. I could sense my own agitation was waiting right there on the edge still. It wouldn't take much to make me pop off again.

After looking up to meet my waiting eyes, she said, "Yeah. I took that cab you saw me get into from the courthouse to the mall, and from there I took an Uber to Abstract. From there, I borrowed Rio's car and drove up the coast a bit to clear my head."

She looked around me to make eye contact with Grant. "That's a really zippy little car, by the way."

My buddy just huffed. "It's a clown car, and I'm buying her something reasonable as soon as we have a few minutes to go car shopping. It's so small it seems dangerous."

Bas spoke up then. "Other than a limo, what car doesn't feel too small to you?"

"I don't know." He gave a boyish shrug. "I was thinking of an SUV of some kind. Once we have kids, we'll need room for all that baby shit I see you guys lugging around."

"Kids?" I asked, eyebrows hiked all the way up to meet my hairline.

"Come again?" Bas snapped his head up from scrolling through email messages.

"Wait, what? Is Rio pregnant?" Hannah seemed thrilled for her friend's big news.

Grant held his hands out over the gang to calm us down. "Settle down. Settle down. No, she's not pregnant. Not yet, anyway." Then he got a sly grin on his full lips and said, "But let's just say we aren't playing our goalie these days."

"That's great news, man." I thumped him on the back a few times. I was truly happy for him that he'd found a woman to spend the rest of his life with, because my friend here always thought he would live out his days alone. That he would always look on from the sidelines.

"So, the Fiat?" Grant looped the conversation back to where we'd started.

Hannah looked sheepish once again. "Last night, when I went to the jobsite downtown, I drove Kendall there. When Mr. Cole found me this morning, we must have driven to his hotel in his car." She looked to me for verification. "Because I don't think I was in any shape to drive. I don't remember driving, at least."

Sebastian really perked up. "Wait a second. Back up the wagon. Who found you?" my friend asked, but what he didn't understand was his normal voice sounded like a bark to most people who weren't used to him.

I could feel Hannah begin to tremble as he spoke to her in his commanding voice.

Again, I took liberties I had no right to and rubbed her back with my free hand and spoke quietly to her. "He's not angry. That's his normal voice. He has no concept of modulation."

I directed my stare to Bas and said, "Jacob Cole was the one who found her this morning, hiding in the stairwell. He drove her back to his hotel and called me from there. Hannah doesn't remember what happened to her cell phone. She must have dropped it somewhere on the property."

Grant interjected. "I'll call security at the jobsite and let them know to alert us if they find a cell phone in that area. That might help figure out how these bastards sent text messages that looked like they came from your phone to hers."

"Two things bother me about this," Bas said as he began to pace back and forth. The motion was a typical stress absorber for our friend.

"What's that?"

"First of all, I told that kid to get permanent housing. Why the hell is he still in a hotel? It makes me feel like he's going to skip town at any minute, and I don't like it."

At first, I was going to protest that the architect's living arrangements weren't really my friend's concern, but then he'd made a valid point.

Sebastian continued. "Secondly, I had a meeting with him early this morning. Wouldn't you think he might have mentioned this?"

Grant fell into pacing behind our boss. "Can we call a spade a spade here?"

When Bas and I both stared at him, not catching on to where he was going with that question, he continued, "The guy is a little strange, right? I wouldn't take anything he says or does personally."

I had to agree with Grant too. Jake was a bit eccentric,

but I had met stranger in my time, so I didn't put too much energy into worrying about it.

"I don't think he's a part of this bullshit, if that's where you were going with that, Bas," I said.

"Nah, it's not that. I just can't figure that guy out. There's something off about him, though. I know that much."

Hannah spoke up finally. "He was very kind to me and very gentle in nature. Almost like he was caring for an injured bird or something."

"What do you mean?" I asked, feeling four different shades of green color my suspicion.

"Well, if I had to imagine which one of you"—she looked pointedly at the three of us—"would be like in that situation . . . No offense, really . . ." She held her hand out in front of her, dragging mine along too. "I imagine it would be a lot rougher around the edges than he was." She shrugged. "He was tender, I guess."

"Isn't that great . . ." I growled and pivoted my body back to face her.

Hannah whipped her head in my direction. "What is your problem?" she hissed in my direction and stood. "Would you rather he have treated me badly?"

"No, of course not," I seethed. "I would rather none of this had happened in the first place."

"Well, it did. And at least Jacob was there to help me." She stared at me defiantly.

I didn't know what she was trying to prove, antagonizing me this way. Time to reestablish who was in charge here.

I backed her up until her back was against the wall and pressed the hard ridge of my body against hers. I bent down so my mouth was right beside her ear and only she could hear what I had to say.

"Watch yourself. Tender or not, Jacob Cole is a fraction of the man it takes to keep you satisfied. Do not wave another man's macho do-gooder bullshit in my face again. You are mine. Do you understand that? Mine." I bit into her neck until she whimpered and then soothed the mark with my tongue. "In case you forgot..." I let an extended beat of silence pass between that and the crux of my comment. "You don't like it tender, beauty."

CHAPTER TWELVE

HANNAH

The same cocky confidence that could be so sexy and alluring could be infuriating and maddening. As Elijah backed away from me, I wanted to both beg for more of his dominant handling and crumble to the ground and throw a tantrum because I was so frustrated.

When had I given over so much control of my own body to this man? Probably after the first time he showed me just how good he could make me feel. After that, I was putty in his hands. I couldn't even defend myself.

Sebastian took control of the conversation as though he were presiding over a board meeting.

"All right, let's be serious here for a few minutes. We've started at least three conversations and didn't finish them. Where is Rio's fucking car?" That one was directed right at me, so everyone in the room turned in my direction to hear the answer.

"I believe it's on one of the side streets at the Edge construction site. I can drive her down there so she can pick it up, or maybe I can have one of the security guys here help me with that task. Although now we have *this* problem." I held up the hand that was still cuffed to Elijah's and rolled my eyes.

"That's something the two of you are going to have to

work out," Bas issued.

"Okay, the next thing, then . . . You need to be brought up to speed"—Sebastian pointed at me—"with the details that we have regarding this guy's abduction." He thumbed over his shoulder to Grant Twombley. "If the people who attacked you last night are the same ones or are working for the same boss, as they call him, we're going to have to come up with a different game plan, because these guys are getting very aggressive." After that comment, he looked to Grant and Elijah, and the three of them agreed with hearty nods.

Elijah offered, "I can catch her up to speed about the kidnappers myself. We don't all have to sit around for that."

Grant chimed in, "Yeah, just make sure you do it this time."

"Don't start with me, dick," Elijah defended. "You have no idea what history she has. She doesn't need extra shit in her head."

"Simmer down, children," Bas chided. "Use your big-boy words."

The rapport these three men had was as special and close as anything I had with my sisters, and it was such a treat to witness. I wished we had spent more time around them and with their women. I would've really enjoyed that, especially given how close I had gotten with Rio lately.

I had so much to think about regarding this man I was literally bound to. There were so many good things about him and about us together. Were the things he decided to keep from me deal breakers, or were they something we could get over?

The problem, though, was that it happened at all. Why didn't he trust me enough to confide in me? We should establish a rule to tell each other anything and everything.

The other person could decide if it was important to them or not.

Maybe if we gave it another try with that rule in place, I could forgive him. How would he respond to having to live by a set of rules? Well, it wasn't a *set* of rules per se. It was just one. Wouldn't that be ironic, given the list of rules he'd handed me when I'd walked through his front door?

I watched quietly from the sidelines while he spoke with his best friends. He was so handsome, commanding, and virile. Elijah Banks was the perfect specimen of a man, and I was so giddy and proud that he was mine.

When he was mine.

But then that stabbing ache came back, right in the middle of my chest. That nagging voice in my head was back too, reminding me he was never really mine. Not all of him, at least. There was a part of him that belonged to another woman because she'd had his child. A part of him lived on with her, as it should. He'd confided in me that he wanted to be a father someday, so I knew if that child turned out to be his, he would not turn his back on him, nor would I want him to.

But what did that situation look like? We rode off into the sunset with another woman's child between us? Only on the weekends and school holidays, of course. I just wasn't sure if it was something I wanted to sign up for.

I wasn't going to be getting clarity on this anytime soon, either. Regardless, it was all premature worrying. First, a paternity test needed to be done. All this worrying, and what if it turned out the child wasn't his?

When there was a lull in the conversation, I asked, "What are your intentions concerning a paternity test?" I had to assume his two best friends knew the whole story about his possible fatherhood. They all seemed to know what each other had for breakfast, for God's sake.

So why did they both snap their attention to Elijah like I'd just given away state secrets?

"She continues to deny that I'm the father and has threatened to go back into hiding if I pursue a paternity test, privately or with the court," Elijah said quietly. But his voice was heavy with another emotion I couldn't exactly identify, but I didn't like it.

"What's going on? What aren't you telling me?" I asked.

"What do you mean?" my man asked. "That's all there is."

Even after his denial, I was skeptical.

"Now is really not the time to bullshit me. The air in this room just got so thick I could cut it with a butter knife. Once again, I'm the odd one out. The three of you know something I don't." I was sure of it.

Elijah turned to me and took both my hands and said, "No, baby, there's nothing else. That's all there is. It's just such a bad topic. No matter which angle I come at it from, someone I care about gets hurt, and I don't like that."

Grant cleared his throat behind us. "All right, man, we're going to shove off. You know where to find me if you need me. Let's all stay vigilant and try to come up with some ideas on where to go from here and what these assholes might want. If they would just tell us what they wanted, we could put this to rest already."

"No shit, right?" Bas added.

"Actually, can you guys sit tight for a little longer?" asked Elijah. "There's one more thing I need to tell you, and it has nothing to do with maritime pirates. But it does have everything to do with Hensley Pritchett." He watched his friends with a hopeful expression.

"Dude, you need to just get rid of that bitch," Grant said. "Erase her from your history book, or you're going to let your future slip through your fingers. How don't you see that?"

"I do see that. And it's scaring me to death. I see it and I'm trying to stop it, and it's happening anyway." He rubbed his face with his palms, and my hand went along for the ride.

I caught a small smile from his tallest friend, and it was like a little reassurance.

"This is all I have left. I need to come clean. Once and for all. I need to tell you all the whole truth so that woman can't lord it over me ever again."

"The whole truth about what?" I asked immediately. I had a really bad feeling in my stomach, and it was the worst emotional whiplash ever. That warm confidence from Grant to this cold dread from Elijah's comment in the blink of an eye.

"I'm just going to be honest here," Grant said. "I hate conversations that start this way. Anyone else? Show of hands?"

Slowly, one by one, we all raised our hands. Even Sebastian finally put his hand up—while rolling his eyes at the absurdity of the whole thing.

"Let's sit down," Elijah said. "This is going to take a while."

We got comfortable in the living room, just off the kitchen, and when everyone was settled, he sat forward a bit and held my tethered hand between his.

He spoke directly to me first. "A lot of these details you won't know, or understand, because our friendship"—he motioned to the men—"started when we were boys. I can fill in what you don't understand later, but I think once I start saying this, it will be better if I just say it all without interruption, okay?"

"All right."

Elijah gripped my hand a bit tighter, angled toward his friends, and took a deep breath. Jesus... Whatever he was about to say, he was most concerned with their reaction.

"None of what I'm about to say changes the man sitting here with you now. It doesn't change the man who works for you or the best friends we've been."

He looked at me and said, "It doesn't change the man who loves you with every beat of his heart. I need you to understand that."

Before I could answer, he looked back to the guys for their reaction to his sincerity.

Grant was the first to reply. "Dude, whatever it is, we have you. You know that. Just tell us."

Bas gave a curt nod, his consent to proceed.

One more deep inhale, and Elijah closed his eyes on the exhale.

Jesus, the suspense was killing me.

"Banks!" Bas barked.

"It's hard. This is really hard," he huffed. "Okay, you remember we were friends when we were really young and then we met again on the streets when we were what? Fourteen? Fifteen? Something like that?"

"Yeah, something like that," Bas agreed.

"I never told you why I couldn't go home. I always said family issues, or some version of that."

"Right," Bas and Grant said in chorus while we all waited for the bomb drop.

"Well, the truth is"—he swallowed so hard I could see his

throat working from my vantage point—"I stabbed my father forty-two times, and he bled to death on the kitchen floor of my family's Bel Air mansion."

ALSO BY VICTORIA BLUE

Shark's Edge Series:
(with Angel Payne)
Shark's Edge
Shark's Pride
Shark's Rise
Grant's Heat
Grant's Flame
Grant's Blaze

★

Elijah's Whim
Elijah's Want
Elijah's Need

Misadventures:
Misadventures with a Book Boyfriend
Misadventures at City Hall

Secrets of Stone Series:
(with Angel Payne)
No Prince Charming
No More Masquerade
No Perfect Princess
No Magic Moment
No Lucky Number
No Simple Sacrifice
No Broken Bond
No White Knight
No Longer Lost

**For a full list of Victoria's other titles,
visit her at VictoriaBlue.com**

ACKNOWLEDGMENTS

Big thanks to the team at Waterhouse Press who has dedicated their time and individual talents to bring you, the loyal readers, this amazing, finished product: Scott Saunders, Meredith Wild, Jon McInerney, Jennifer Becker, Haley Boudreaux, Yvonne Ellis, Kurt Vachon, Jesse Kench, and Amber Maxwell. I'm also thankful for the Waterhouse proofing, copyediting, and formatting teams. Thank you for your keen eye and attention to detail.

My dearest Megan Ashley—Thank you for keeping my professional life organized and running smoothly. Your happiness is my happiness, and every laugh we share makes my day that much brighter. You are one of the most beautiful people I know. XOXO

To every single member of Victoria's Book Secrets—I can't express how much I love each and every sister in our group. We've grown into a fabulous, caring family. The love and support you show me and one another makes me so proud to call you mine.

Lastly, a special thank you to Amy Bourne for your love and support through life's ups and downs. Also, thank you for reading early versions of my stories and fairly critiquing my ideas. You have no idea how much I value your opinion. I love you with my whole heart. XOXO

ABOUT VICTORIA BLUE

International bestselling author Victoria Blue lives in her own portion of the galaxy known as Southern California. There, she finds the love and life-sustaining power of one amazing sun, two unique and awe-inspiring planets, and four indifferent yet comforting moons. Life is fantastic and challenging and every day brings new adventures to be discovered. She looks forward to seeing what's next!

Visit her at VictoriaBlue.com